Raine

Ty Sam-Davis

DEDICATION

To the kids that struggle to get their next meal,
have been abandoned by drug addicted
parents/relatives, or have been abused.
Fight to survive.
The world needs you.
Please don't give up.
This book is for you.
.

CHAPTER 1

Moonlight shined through a sheet of dust decorating the rickety window as loud pounding on the front door rattled his windowpane. A crack started at the top and stopped right in the middle of the glass. He was sure if the knocks continued, the crack would split the glass into tiny pieces.

Wind whistled through the opening causing his body to shiver. He pulled the dingy blanket up to his neck and flipped on his back. He had a jacket on but that still did not keep the ice-cold floor from chilling his body.

BANG.

The pounding continued. Raine wouldn't dare get off the floor and answer it. Besides, he knew every visitor's knock. He came every weekend at around this time. Raine slapped his palm against the floor to scare away rats and noticed a light moving through the hall.

"Hold on, beating on my door like the police."

Raine's door opened and in walked his mother.

When she shined the flashlight into the room, Raine squeezed his eyes shut and pretended to be asleep.

She slammed the door closed, making the windowpane rattle once more. Their muffled voices trailed through the quiet house. It was one in the morning and Raine was trying to get some sleep, but his mother's company and the scurrying rats would not allow him to relax.

Raine moved under the window and pulled the small sketchbook and pen from his jacket pocket. He angled the book to get enough light from the night sky to see the pages. Flipping open the cover he ran his thumb over the note.

In your life, there will be hard times and problems so bad it may seem like you've been buried under it with no way out: fight to pull yourself out, fight to reach a happy place again, and fight to survive. Happy Birthday Rainbow. Love, Mama.

Latisha bought him the sketchbook five years ago for his eighth birthday. Five years ago, he had a bed. Five years ago, the lights and water worked.

"You got that?" His mother asked her visitor followed by her room door slamming shut.

Raine rolled the dull pencil lead over the page. A feminine face soon formed with large dimples in her cheeks. Her smile traveled up to her eyes causing them to become slits. He ran his hand over the sketch making a smudge of grey under her eyes, next to her mouth, and along her hairline. Satisfied that the sketch now resembled the woman that walked the dark hallway at night, he closed the book and grabbed his blanket. He held his spot against the wall and waited for day light.

∞

Pickup games ran on each court. A convoy of cars slowly drove by the court filled with neighborhood kids. Music blared from the car speakers and the chrome rims sparkled in the sun. Kids ran to the fence to get a better look.

"That's my car right there," said a little kid, pointing at a dark green car with gold rims that poked out.

King had climbed the highest on the fence to get the best view. "Raine, come see The Family roll through."

Raine dribbled the ball off to the side while he waited for his turn on the court. He was looking forward to playing a quick game to keep his mind off his growling stomach. He gave a hurried glance in their direction, then returned his attention back to the ball. Watching the local gang show off their cars was the last thing he wanted to do.

"I can see from here," said Raine.

"That's game. Who got next?" yelled Lewis.

King jumped down, his long braids settling on his shoulders. "We got next. Come on, Raine."

Raine sighed. He hoped the guys on the other court had finished before Lewis. He wanted to shoot a relaxing game of hoops not go back and forth with the *golden boy*. Raine wiped cool sweat from his forehead and onto his shirt. When he saw Lewis looking his way, he tugged at the hem of his shorts which stopped high above his knees.

"Look at this clown. I know y'all can't ball." Lewis pointed at Raine's shorts, getting a few laughs.

Raine shook his leg and pulled his shorts down as far as they could go without showing his underwear. He crossed his arms behind his back and stared at the ground, causing Lewis to laugh again.

Raine pushed Lewis and grabbed the ball. "Shut up."

Raine dribbled between his legs doing his best to shake Lewis, and if he fell that would be even better. He forgot about his stomach pain and set out to embarrass Lewis.

"Who has *short* shorts? Raine has *short* shorts," mocked Lewis.

Raine gave him a hard bump, knocking Lewis' tall but skinny frame to the ground, and making the lay-up.

"Foul," yelled Lewis.

"No fouls in street ball," said Raine.

"Yeah, stop whining," said King.

Lewis snatched the ball and ran to take it out. He passed the ball to his teammate and called for the ball back. He shot a three and made it.

Lewis clapped his hands. "Let's go!"

Raine groaned. Embarrassing Lewis was going to be harder than he thought. He passed the ball to

King to take it out.

"Ball," said Raine.

King passed him the ball and he pulled up for a three. The ball bounced off the rim and into Lewis' hand.

"Ugh," said Raine.

Lewis laid the ball up. "Too easy."

"Come on, Raine. Don't let him get in yo head," said King.

Raine dribbled around and tried to drive to the basket. Each time Lewis cut him off, Raine got mad at his hands for not dribbling faster and his feet for not moving with more skill. Especially, against someone like Lewis. The wannabe with married parents and a house in the suburbs.

Raine tried another three and *swish*, all net.

"Come on, Lewis. Defend your man," yelled Lewis' teammate.

"What do you think I'm doing?" said Lewis.

"I guess those tiny shorts give him superpowers," said Lewis' teammate. He reached out and gave Raine dap.

Lewis punched him on the arm. "Get back on defense."

Raine and King were two points away from winning the game. Raine scored most of the points on Lewis with ease. Lewis moved closer to Raine and tried his best to defend him.

Raine laughed. "You can't guard me."

He faked a shot and dribbled around Lewis. Raine was about to shoot, but Lewis slapped his wrist and pushed him. King caught the ball and passed it back to Raine.

"Shoot it," King yelled.

Raine shot the ball and watched as it fell through the net.

"Game! That's my lil' *brudda*," said King; they slapped hands and bumped chests.

"Stinky crack baby," mumbled Lewis. He snatched his shirt off the ground and walked towards the gate.

Raine's stomach turned. He wasn't a crack baby and he was tired of telling everyone to stop calling him that. His smile dropped as the words echoed through his head. He could walk away and pretend he didn't hear Lewis or make him regret those words. Raine dropped the ball and ran over to him, punching Lewis in the face. Lewis fell to the ground, but that didn't stop Raine's attack. He wasn't scary, and he wasn't a crack baby.

"Let him go, Raine." King smirked, and patted Raine on the back. "We're out."

Raine walked over Lewis, making sure to give him a final kick before leaving. He didn't understand why Golden Boy came to their park anyway. Raine knew there were parks closer to Lewis' suburb that looked better. He was sure Lewis only came to make fun of him.

Instead of taking his mind off his stomach, the basketball game made him hungrier and now he had a headache. Raine left the court and headed home for a nap.

∞

Raine removed his forearm from his face and groaned. He felt like the sun was tapping on his window. Blinds or a curtain would have helped, but that was the least of his worries. He planned to take a nap but slept through the night. At least, he didn't have to worry about finding food while asleep.

He sat up and rubbed his back. The hard floor made his back and side ache. He crept to a stand and stretched his arms high above his head. He grabbed his blanket off the floor, rolled it up and toss it in the corner. Raine walked into the bathroom and grabbed his bucket to get ready for school. Every morning, he went into his neighbor's yard and filled up the bucket using her hose.

He crept through the backdoor careful not to wake his mother's company. He eased the bathroom door shut. Every creek the door made caused his heart to race. He splashed water on his face and stared into the broken mirror. He started twisting his hair two years ago. Raine was tired of hearing he needed a haircut and being called nappy headed. He didn't have food or decent clothes. *How do people expect me to get a haircut every other week?*

Raine went into his backyard and retrieved his school clothing. The clothes were stiff from being hand washed in cold water and hung on the clothesline to dry. He grabbed his book sack off the floor after getting dressed and headed for the bus stop.

He treaded toward the front door but halted when he saw Jackson blocking the door. Raine attempted to walked around him, but Jackson stuck his arm out and blocked his path. Jackson placed his cigarette in his mouth. He grabbed Raine's collar and pushed him against the wall.

"Let me go," said Raine.

Jackson smirked. He blew smoke into Raine's face. "And if I don't?"

Raine clenched the strap on his book sack and waved away the smoke. The motion brought his attention to his arm. He had cigarette burns decorating his arm from their encounter last week. Raine wanted to reach back and land a blow right into Jackson's nose, like he did Lewis. But Jackson would toss him around with ease. He always bragged about being a champion boxer. Jackson was skinny, but he could land a jab that would make Raine crumble to the floor.

He pushed Jackson's hand down and scowled at him. His mother's room door opened, and she stumbled out.

"You headed to school," she asked, with her eyes half closed.

Raine, feeling confident that Jackson wouldn't hit him in his mother's presence, gave Jackson a bump and headed for the door.

"Punk," Jackson said, as Raine closed the door.

Raine jogged down the steps and crossed the street towards the bus stop. The sun seemed less intimidating with half of its body hidden behind morning mist.

"Wait up," said King.

Raine glanced over at King and then himself. His polo shirt was faded to a light red and his khaki shorts were too small. He sagged the shorts a little because if he pulled them up to his waist properly, they were high above his knees. Raine's dreads stood tall on his head and the front desperately needed an edge up.

King's shirt was bright red. His khaki pants had creases from his mom ironing them. His hair was braided in zig-zags and laid neatly past his shoulders.

"Did you sketch anything this weekend?"

Raine handed him the sketchbook he'd stolen from the dollar store. He kept the leather covered sketchbook his mom bought in the inner pocket of his pants. He was careful to only sketch meaningful art in that one.

"What does it mean?"

"Whatever you want it to," said Raine.

Raine had sketched a prison cell filled with easels. He couldn't wait to show his art teacher the sketch. He knew she would want him to recreate the sketch on a canvas, something he was looking forward to completing.

"I hit up Dolla this weekend about us joining The Family. He said we need to put in work first."

"We? I don't wanna join a gang. That's your thing," said Raine.

"It's *our* thing if it puts money in our pockets."

Raine frowned. "You get money from your mama whenever you ask."

"She wanna know too much. What I need it for? What I'm gonna do with it? I wanna make my own money."

"I'm good on that."

King handed Raine a bag of food. "Look, just come with me. You don't have to join. Be my backup."

Raine snatched his sketch book from King, pushed away the food and walked toward the bus stop. His stomach growled and twisted, stopping his steps. He knew if King didn't show up at school, he wouldn't have anything to eat. His mother never filled out the paperwork to get free lunch and there was no way he could pay, even if it was only a dollar a day.

King grabbed his arm. "I need someone to watch my back. Someone I can trust."

Raine adjusted his book sack and glanced at the bus stop. He knew once approached, The Family would expect loyalty. Raine decided he would stay outside while King handled his business to avoid confusion.

"All right, but don't mention anything about me joining."

The pair treaded down the avenue to a daiquiri shop owned by Dolla. Each step Raine took, made his feet heavier or maybe it was his heart or his brain. His mother's words replayed in his head. *Fight to survive.* Survival for Raine meant avoiding the gang and going to school.

CHAPTER 2

Outside the daiquiri shop, old school cars lined the parking lot. An old school car on 28-inch rims burned off green smoke from the tires. Raine leaned on the wall and watched the dealers shoot dice off to the side of the car show. They tossed money on the ground like it was nothing, arguing after each dice roll.

"I'm getting a car like that," said King. He bumped into Raine while gawking at the cars.

"Why are they here so early?" asked Raine.

"Dolla runs a tight ship," said King.

In the corner of his eyes, he saw a girl leaning against a car. The car had orange paint that shined like candy and made her dark-brown skin glow.

"Come on," said King. He held the door open for Raine to join him.

"I'm good. Handle yours. I'll be out here."

"How are you gonna have my back from outside the door?" asked King.

Raine glanced past him. He knew walking into the shop was a risk, but his best friend needed him to have his back. Raine was sure King would do the same for him. Anytime he knocked, King would feed him. He walked into the shop and stood off to the side while King waited in line.

"Remember what I told you," said Raine.

The cashier smacked on a piece of gum. "What can I get you?"

"Um. I'm here to see Dolla," said King. He avoided eye contact with the cashier and began tapping on the counter.

The cashier's eyes squinted. She waved her hands adorned with long nails. "Never heard of him."

King tried to look around her. "He told me to see him. I'm trying to be down with The Family."

Raine shook his head. He knew coming with King was a bad idea. He was making himself look suspect.

The cashier stepped away and walked to the back. Raine gave King a quick nod and pulled out his sketchbook. He saw beads of sweat form on King's forehead.

She appeared a few minutes later. "Come on."

King followed her and paused. He mouthed *please* to Raine then waited for him to join. King gave Raine the look. The *look* made Raine feel sorry for him or indebted to him for always giving him food. Raine didn't like feeling obligated to go along with King but he felt trapped.

Which was why he shoved his sketchbook into his back pocket and followed them. Pass the mixing machines, they came into a concrete warehouse.

Raine's worn shoes squeaked against the scratched-up floors. Unlike the air-conditioned shop, the back room was filled with heat that engulfed their faces as soon as they entered. A huge fan circulated warm air around the room. The cashier left them in a hurry and treaded back the way she came.

"Where is everyone?" asked King. He walked into the middle of the room and rolled the balls around a pool table.

Raine's eyes scanned the room, dancing around every corner and angle. He stayed off to the side hoping to go unnoticed. The room was quiet, too quiet. He backed into a corner and continued to scan.

"You police?" said a voice from behind King.

"Na...No. I'm not police. I'm only thirteen." King backed away from the boy. He had to be a senior in high school because he towered over them.

"Look how scared he looks. Boy about to pee his pants," said another boy, with a Saints jersey on and a gold chain around his neck.

His chain had the number twenty-two on it, and it dangled around his neck almost putting Raine in a trance. He stood next to the other tall figure.

Raine stumbled into the middle of the room after being pushed farther inside by a third teen. Raine yanked away from him and frowned.

"He thinks he tough," said the third boy, pointing at Raine. He had a scar above his lip.

He pushed Raine down to the floor. Raine knew there was no way he could win. Especially, since the boy with the jersey on had made his way over to him. He could either cower away or fight.

Raine jumped up from the floor and brought his fists up to his face. The teens punched and kicked him all over. Raine was no match for them, but he hugged the one with the scar's waist and threw punches to try and defend himself. Every time they dropped him with a punch, Raine got back up. Even though he tried to protect his face, he still got punched there. His face was stinging from the contact.

"Ok, they've had enough."

A figured emerged from a side door. He had tattoos decorating his face, but they were barely visible because of his dark complexion. Raine did notice the dollar bill tattooed in the center of his neck. His heart raced as the infamous Dolla walked up to them.

Raine spat blood on the floor and held his shirt up to stop blood from falling from his nose. His body felt sore, like after one of Jackson's beatings.

King was curled up in a ball and whimpering. His cries did not fill the room but they were loud enough for the people in the room to notice. Although, Raine wanted to cry, he refused to do so in a room filled with members of The Family.

Dolla shook his head at King and treaded over to Raine. Raine brought his fists back up but backed away.

"Chill youngin', I'on want beef." Dolla threw his hands up and smiled at the teens that handed Raine his beat down. Raine dropped his hands to his side but stayed on guard.

Dolla held his hand out to Raine. Raine placed his hands into his pockets instead. He didn't see anything funny about being beaten to a pulp by guys twice his size.

"I like the way you handled yourself. You got your butt kicked but you didn't run or cry like a punk." Dolla looked over at King. King wiped tears away before dropping his head.

"You wanna be down?" asked Dolla.

"Na, that's his thing. I just came with him," said Raine.

Dolla reached into his pocket and pulled out a roll of money. He flipped back five hundred dollars. Dolla walked over to King and handed him the money.

King quickly snatched the money from Dolla. "Thanks, man."

Dolla swaggered over to Raine, dressed in expensive shoes and designer jeans. He counted off eight hundred dollars and stretched out his hand to Raine. Raine stared at the money.

Dolla's brow raised. "This is eight hundred dollars. Gon' and take it."

Raine looked down at his shoes. His white sneakers were yellow from washing them too many times. There was a hole on the toe and thread loose on the side. That money would be enough for food, shoes, and clothes.

"I'm good." Raine looked around the room. "Can I leave?"

Dolla rubbed his chin. He and the boy with the

scar above his lip exchanged nods. Dolla gestured toward the door.

Raine stormed through the front door of the shop. He glanced down at his uniform shirt. The shirt looked tie dyed with faded red patches and spots of bright red from his bloody nose.

"Raine, wait up." King limped to him.

Raine grabbed King by his collar. "That was stupid! We could've been killed."

King pushed him away and fixed his collar. "I made five hundred dollars. He offered you more than me. Why didn't you take it, stupid?"

"Stupid? I'm not the stupid one, you are," yelled Raine.

"How?"

"You got five hundred dollars for what? You went in there for a job but didn't ask for one. Now you owe Dolla and I'm not with owing people."

"Whatever," said King, as he counted his money. "You want something to eat?"

Raine decided he needed some time away from King. "I'm good."

"I'll hit you up later. Thanks for having my back."

Raine headed the opposite direction to the levee. The only place he could clear his mind. Cars sped by, echoing off the road and creating a rhythm. The sky was clear of clouds. It would have been a beautiful day if he wasn't trying to stop a nosebleed and limping with each step. Raine leaned forward and grabbed his stomach, feeling the urge to vomit but his empty stomach prevented the action. His eyes watered as he hurled clear liquid. He wiped his mouth and forged on; the sight of the levee eased his mind.

Raine followed the path to the top of the levee and took a seat on the bench, tossing his bloody shirt next to him. The shirt reminded him of his dumb decision to go with King instead of school.

He pulled out the leather covered sketchbook and flipped to a new page. A bandana caught in the wind blew onto the page. Then a handgun, like the one on Dolla's side. *Bang.* Sparks flew from the gun and grey bullets littered the page. The Bullets blurred into money. The money trickled down into drugs. A lady extended her arms, giving all her attention to the drugs, ignoring a crying boy beside her. Raine drew more details in the sketch until he relaxed. He headed home to scrub the blood from his shirt but bloody shirt or not, he was looking forward to the art demonstration at school tomorrow.

∞

Raine walked into class clenching his side. He would have stayed home to heal but today was the big day. His art teacher, Mrs. Kathy, got a well-known painter, Camille Savoy, to do a live painting in their classroom. Camille was one of Raine's favorite painters. She was from New Orleans and painted daily city life from second lines to violence in the city. He heard King's loudmouth from the door, causing him to groan.

"You already know. I was throwing them off me

left and right. I had about three of them on me," said King.

"Settle down. Let's begin our lesson," said the teacher, Mr. Riker.

Raine eased into his seat and peered at the clock. He had two more classes to get through before art class. King quickly handed him a brown bag and continued to the back of the class. Raine opened the bag and pulled out an apple, eating it in a couple of bites. He pulled out the sandwich but put it back inside for lunch. His stomach growled at the sight of the sandwich.

"Pssst," said King, and pointed to the door.

In walked the girl from the parking lot at the daiquiri shop. Her eyes dashed around the room before resting on Mr. Riker. She gave him a note.

"Well, looks like we have a new student. Class this is…?"

She turned to the teacher. "Laila Mitchell."

"Laila, take the empty seat over there."

"She fine," Raine whispered. He gawked at her curly hair and dark skin until he realized she was heading his way, causing him to sit up straight. Raine turned his attention to his hands when she neared his desk.

"How you gonna give the new girl the seat by Raine's dirty self," said Lewis, making the class laugh.

Raine raised his head and made eye contact with Laila. She looked at Lewis and then at him. He looked away and tried to get rid of the stomach-turning pain he felt when someone called him stinky or dirty. They always called him dirty. Even though he bathed every morning as best as he could with a bucket full of freezing water and hand soap. He washed his clothes every other day. Some of the stains stayed put because he washed them without detergent. But he did not *stink*. He made sure of that.

"Lewis, refrain from any further outburst," said Mr. Riker.

Raine shot out of his seat, causing the desk to rattle. He walked to the back of the class where Lewis sat smirking with his arms folded.

"Why don't you mind your business?" asked Raine. He didn't understand why Lewis always worried about his appearance.

Lewis frowned. "Why don't you mind... some soap and water?"

Raine ignored his teacher's pleas to return to his seat. He grabbed Lewis by the collar and pulled him out of the desk. He threw punches until his classmates pulled him off.

"Go to the front office now," said Mr. Riker.

Raine grabbed his stuff and marched out of the classroom, leaving most of the desks scattered around the room.

He was suspended for three days and had to spend the rest of the day in detention because the school couldn't reach his mother. Of course, Lewis was only given two days in detention.

Raine stared at the wall inside the cubicles and imagined what type of art Camille painted for his art class. He missed the art show and now he had to worry about finding food for the next three days, since he couldn't return to school.

∞

Raine was lying on his back watching the room spin. He closed his eyes and shook his head to ward off dizziness. His sketchbook rested on his stomach and his pencil was clenched between his teeth. He started a sketch to keep his mind distracted, but anime characters soon found burgers and fries in their hands. Eventually, food items littered the page.

He hadn't had a decent meal in about three days. He forgot all about his sandwich when he went to teach Lewis a lesson. Now, he wished he would've at least grabbed the sandwich after kicking his butt. His mother hadn't been home all day and even if she was, she wouldn't have food.

He staggered to his feet, dragging himself to the kitchen, hoping something magically appeared since he checked two hours ago. An empty baking soda box lie on the shelf. He ate the lumps of dried powder hours ago. He grabbed his stomach and closed the fridge. Raine dropped to the floor and laid his head on the cool tile. He wanted to cry but what good would that do? He would still be hungry. His head ached, and his stomach demanded food.

He got up from the floor and headed to King's house. The first few steps were always the worst. The sun showed no mercy and made his head spin more. He dipped his head and hurried across the street.

Raine walked up the porch and the smell of food made him more desperate. He knocked on the door, lightly. There was a slight chance King would hear him and not Kia. After getting no answer he knocked harder.

"What," yelled Kia, King's mother. She had a cooking spoon in her hand with food stuck on it.

Red beans, he thought.

Kia stared at him and sighed when he didn't speak right away. Raine looked away from the spoon. Her glare made him want to turn around and go back home.

"Is King home?"

"King is playing the game with his *friends*," she replied.

Raine turned to walk away. He needed food, but he refused to beg her to call King.

"King!" she yelled.

She crossed her arms over her chest and peered over at him. "Lewis told me you punched him. Always in trouble because your maw don't watch you." She stormed away, letting the screen door slam in his face.

"Bald head," Raine mumbled.

King appeared in the door eating a bowl of cereal. "What's up, Raine?"

"My mama didn't make groceries."

"I'll be back," said King.

A few minutes later, King and a few other boys from school walked out onto the porch. Raine eyed Lewis until King tapped him.

"Let's go," said King.

King told the guys he would talk to them later. Raine hadn't planned on walking in the heat. He was weak, and his energy was draining with each step. Raine didn't see why King didn't grab him a plate from his house. *Kia probably told him not to.*

"It's too hot to be…"

"What's up now?" asked King.

Raine looked over and saw him staring at two boys sitting in a dirt lot on milk crates.

Raine grabbed King's shirt. "What are you doing?"

"Chill out and have my back."

"You acting hard because you got him with you? I just slapped you and you walked away," said one of the boys.

"What up then?" asked King.

"Hold this."

The boy handed his gun to his friend then approached King. They rotated around in a circle shuffling their feet, adjusting their fists. Raine's stomach roared causing the boy to turn around.

"What was that? Ay, watch my back," the boy told his friend.

Raine took a seat on one of the milk crates and dropped his head in his hands. He was heated. All he wanted was food and King brought him down into gang territory to watch him shuffle around in the dirt. Raine looked up when he heard rocks shuffling. The boy knocked King to the ground and was standing over him landing blows.

"Let him get up," said Raine.

The boy ignored him and continued to pounce on King.

"Raine, get him off me!" King yelled.

Raine walked over and pushed the boy. The boy's friend rushed Raine and pummeled him with punches. Raine's arms felt like spaghetti. He barely had enough energy to swing.

"Hey, stop all that mess," yelled an old lady, sitting on her porch. "Wait a second. Let me call the police."

The two boys backed away while Raine and King did the same. When they were a few blocks away, Raine shoved King.

"You should've told me you went there to fight."

"My bad." He handed Raine ten dollars. "Go get some food."

Raine snatched the money and wiped his bloody lip. Like always, King looked out for him. Today was only his first day of his three-day suspension. Raine headed to the corner store to buy cans of soup. That would last him throughout his suspension

CHAPTER 3

Raine slammed the fridge shut and walked into his mother's room. He pushed cigarette butts and foil paper around the dresser hoping to find money.

"Never have any money."

He was about to leave but decided to check under her mattress. He snatched the wrinkled dollar from between the mattress. He grabbed a colored pencil from his booksack and headed out the front door. Today was his last suspension day. The cans of soup would've lasted but he was starving and ate more than he should've.

"Give me all your money."

Raine pushed King away and laughed.

"I scared you, didn't I?" asked King.

"No indeed. I knew it was you," said Raine.

"Don't forget to lock your door."

Raine shook his head. "Nothing in there to steal. Trust me."

King boxed around him. "Where are you going?"

"To make some groceries."

King rubbed his hands together. "You know I'm down. What's the plan this time?"

Raine held up the dollar. "This."

"A dollar? Mr. Johnson ain't letting us in the store with a dollar."

"That's why I'm gonna turn it into a Benjamin with this colored pencil."

Raine sat on a bench outside the store and drew on the dollar. He blew away the green pencil shavings and held the transformed dollar up to King.

"Let me see it from a distance." King backed up and used his hands as a frame. "Looks like a hundred dollars from here."

"Good let's go."

King snatched the money from Raine's hand. "We should go into business changing money."

"Give it back, dummy. Before you mess it up."

"Give it back," said King, making sure to make his voice high pitched and whiny.

Raine pulled the door open and stopped when a broom handle blocked his path.

"Uh-huh. You ain't comin' in my store, Storm, and take Prince with you," said Mr. Johnson. He tied his apron in preparation of Raine's antics.

"My name is Raine and he's King. You know that, Mr. Johnson."

He poked them with the broom. "I don't care if it's Purple Rain, get out."

"Ouch, old man," said King.

"I got money," said Raine. He held up the dollar

using his thumb to shield the zeros.

Mr. Johnson poked Raine again. "I know some po' old lady missing her first check. Hurry up and get what you need, and you better not steal boy, ya hear?"

"Yes, sir." Raine smiled and rushed to grab a bag.

King glanced back at Mr. Johnson. He was behind the counter reading a newspaper. "What's next?"

"I'm going to get some stuff and then give him the money."

Raine walked around the aisle and found everything he needed in one spot. "It never fails. Every time I come here, I find everything I need in the same spot. I never have to look for it."

"That is weird. You might have a stalker," said King.

"Whatever," Raine glanced at Mr. Johnson. "I got everything. Let's do this."

"I love you, man," said King, wrapping him in a hug.

Raine laughed. "Get off me."

He walked to the front and allowed Mr. Johnson to ring everything up. King was holding the door open, pretending to talk to someone.

"Hello, Raine," said Mrs. Johnson.

"Evening," said Raine.

Mrs. Johnson winked her hazel eyes at Raine, kissed Mr. Johnson on the cheek and then disappeared through the side door.

Mrs. Johnson was the opposite of her husband.

She always smiled making her hazel eyes glow, and she was always nice to him when he came. Raine was sure she knew about him stealing each time, but she never gave him a hard time about it. Raine wondered what she looked like when she was younger. Mr. Johnson knocked on the counter. "Stop watching my wife, young blood."

Raine laughed. He placed the money on the counter and eyed the door, tapping his hand on the counter while Mr. Johnson scanned the items.

"Okay, total is twenty-two dollars."

He didn't like stealing from Mr. Johnson, but he had no other choice. Mr. Johnson never called the police…well, he didn't stick around to find out. He knew if he stole food from one of the supermarkets he would be arrested before leaving the store. He had a better chance getting away from Mr. Johnson.

Raine grabbed the two bags and ran out the door. "Keep the change!"

He ran pass King and turned the corner. Mr. Johnson was out the store yelling at them.

"Hold on, my heart," said King.

Raine slowed and let him catch up. He laughed at King gasping for air. "You're slow anyway. How do you score touchdowns?"

"Shut up, punk. I'm running with slippers on," said King. His slippers were sideways and halfway off his feet.

"My bad. I didn't notice you had those on. You're lucky Mr. Johnson didn't catch you."

"No, he's lucky. I beat old men up too," said King. He punched around Raine's face.

"Stop, man. You're gonna make me drop the bag."

King laughed. "Are you coming back to school this week?"

"No. I come back Monday."

"The whole school is talking about your fight. Did you see Lewis' black eye?"

Raine shrugged. "I don't care."

"I'll see you later," said King; he dashed across the street to his house.

Raine already knew what he wanted to eat first, two tuna fish sandwiches. He paused upon spotting his mother sitting on the floor, staring at a collection of dust on the ceiling. She groaned and tried to stand. Raine dropped the bags on the floor and went over to her.

"Drink some water," he said.

Latisha knocked the water bottle down. "I don't want water."

Her eyes dashed toward the door. "How much this stuff cost? You have the receipt?"

Raine snatched the water bottle off the floor and grabbed bags. He walked into the kitchen with her on his track.

"Raine…"

"No. You're not selling our food."

She smiled showing her yellow tinted teeth. "Mama will buy more. Look, you can take a few things out the bag."

"I said *no*." He grabbed a rusted butter knife out

the drawer and struggled with opening the can of tuna.

"Rainbow…"

He needed every item to stretch for at least a week. Her little tricks used to work on him as a child but now she couldn't trick him. If he let her sell one item, then she wouldn't stop until all of it was gone.

"No, *Latisha.*"

He finally got the can open and fixed his sandwich. He grabbed the bags and headed to his room. He heard the door slam, once again rattling the windowpane. Raine placed the bags into his book sack and ate lunch.

After eating, Raine headed to the levee but not before leaving a few items of food on the counter for his mother to sell. A full stomach required a new art piece. He strolled down the street with his pencil behind his ear and his sketchbook in his hand.

A car hopped the curb and jerked to a stop, causing the breaks to squeak. Raine jumped in the grass to avoid being hit.

"Raine?"

A boy walked up to him with his hand on his waist band revealing a "The Family" tattoo on his arm.

"No," said Raine, placing his sketchbook inside his pocket in preparation of running off.

"You know why I'm here," said the boy. "Don't think about running."

"I don't know," said Raine. "You threatening

me?"

The boy frowned. "Threatening?"

"Yeah, you tried to hit me with that car."

The boy laughed. "My bad. I was trying to park my car. You think I'm gonna dent it by hitting your long head?"

"Your car? You need driving lessons," said Raine.

The boy shrugged. "I can't get lessons. I'm not old enough. Look, Dolla wants you on the team. I can drive you to him."

"Boy, you can't drive!"

"Don't worry about all that. Do you wanna get down with us or not?"

"Why would I do that? All y'all do is sell drugs and break up families," said Raine.

Offended, the boy rushed up to Raine. "Do we make the feens cop? Is there a gun to their heads? Don't blame us for supplying the demand."

Raine looked away. He was right. No one made his mother get high. She chose to become a drug addict. When the boy rushed up to him, he recognized him. He was the same boy that beat him up at the shop.

"You look like you can use the money. You put in work and never have to worry." He pulled a roll of money from his pockets.

"What would I have to do?"

"Same thing I do. Follow Dolla's orders. Simple."

He could use the money, but Raine didn't want to be in a gang. There was no way he would sell drugs and ruin another family.

"I'm good," said Raine.

"Cool. You wanna walk around in yo' little brother's clothes and dirty shoes." He shrugged. "If you like it, then I love it."

He walked to his car, one that most adults couldn't afford. He had the seat leaned so far back that only his knuckles on the steering wheel were visible. Raine headed back home, no longer in the mood to draw. Thanks to King, The Family knew his name and face.

∞

Raine sat on his porch drawing. He tried to be out of the house when his mother had company. The sun shined, and buses littered the street dropping kids off. Raine was on a third sketch of his father, or what he imagined he may look like.

The first image was a heavy-set guy, the second was slender and had long dreadlocks, and the third one resembled him but with short hair.

"What's up?" King walked up and slapped hands with Raine.

"Chillin'."

King took a seat next to him. "I wish I was home all day. School's boring."

"I'm bored at home too."

"I wouldn't be. You wanna come to my house?"

Raine raised a brow. There was no way Kia would let him inside.

"She isn't home. She's shopping with her friends. You know that takes hours."

Raine closed his book and followed King to his house.

"I bought some new clothes with the money Dolla gave me."

"You should've given it back. Dolla is bad news."

Raine peeped around before lightly closing the door behind them. King pushed him farther inside.

"My mama is the same height as you and you're scared." King laughed before getting back on the subject of Dolla. "I'll take money from the boogie man."

"Your mama's mean. What happens if Dolla comes looking for his money?"

"That was chump change to him," said King.

King had his clothes laid out on the bed and shoes on the floor. Above his bed was the only picture he had of his dad. Raine always looked at the picture and wondered if he ever took any pictures with his father.

The picture read: Royal age 22 and King age 5

Royal and King had on matching Nike track suits with Jordan shoes on. Royal had on gold jewelry that he draped over King's neck.

King walked up next to him. "My dad was the first one in New Orleans with that kind of car. I'm gonna have my own car soon."

"How? When you spent all your money on shoes?" asked Raine.

"I'm gonna save next time."

Raine imagined being in King's position and knew he would buy food and turn on the water with his money.

"King, come help me with these bags."

Raine's eyes stretched. "She's home," he whispered.

"Calm down, scary lil' boy," King said, and laughed.

Raine pushed him. "Stop laughing."

"Coming," said King.

King headed out the room and tried to close the door. Raine caught it and walked out behind him. He didn't want to face Kia, but he didn't want to hide in the room like a criminal either.

"I bought those snacks you wanted," said Kia. She paused when Raine walked into the front room.

"Didn't I tell you not to have company while I'm not here?"

"It's only Raine," said King.

"Only Raine my tail. What are you doing in my house, little boy?" Kia looked around King and turned her nose up at Raine.

"I was leaving," Raine responded.

"Mrs. Boudreaux called and told me about y'all fighting the other day. King, you know better than to be a follower, fighting like you don't have any sense."

Raine's eyes dashed from King and back to his mother. King grabbed the bags and passed Kia, ignoring her.

"You're gonna end up just like your father, having his friends' backs was more important than us. You wanna die behind another person's bull?"

she yelled at King.

Raine walked towards the door. The fight was King's fault and she was blaming him.

"Don't come back to my house," said Kia.

Raine pushed the door open, hitting it on the wall and stormed down the steps.

Kia yelled. "Push my door open like that again. Always fighting and causing trouble," she said to his back.

Raine ignored her but Kia's words left a lingering sting. He walked into his house and into his room, punching the wall until his fist was sore.

His room door opened, and Latisha walked in. Her hair was a mess and her clothes were dirty. "What's all that noise?"

Raine had taken a seat on the floor and was rubbing his fist.

"Let me see your hand."

"Get away from me," said Raine. He rushed past her and went into the backyard.

CHAPTER 4

Raine's suspension was over and he was happy to be back at school. He stared at the back of Laila's head all morning, wondering if her hair was as soft as it looked. He was relieved to finish third period. He couldn't wait to get to art class to see Camille's painting.

King rushed over to him outside the lunchroom. "Here, you can take my lunch. I'm sneaking off campus."

"Why?" asked Raine.

"Don't worry about it. Eat up."

Raine shrugged and took the two bags of lunch. He was hungry, and King came at the right moment.

Raine decided to eat outside at his favorite table. He had survived the first few classes and was excited about going to art class after lunch. He paused upon spotting a female at his table.

"Shake the spot," he said.

Laila stopped eating her sandwich and frowned. "Who are you talking to?"

"This is my table."

"I don't see your name here," she replied.

"I always sit here."

She moved her books. "Sit down because I'm not leaving."

"You want me to sit next to you? You didn't hear? I'm the dirty one."

"Okay, *Dirty One.* Sit down or let me eat in peace." Laila waved her hand dismissing him and resumed eating.

He snatched up his lunch and walked towards the door.

"That's what I thought," she said, to his back.

He ate in the gym and drew until the bell rang ending lunch. Raine walked towards his art class but was stopped in the hall.

"Raine, did you hear about your friend?" asked Kesha.

"Who?"

"King. The Family snatched him up."

As Mrs. Kathy motioned for Raine to head inside art class, he looked at the classroom door then the parking lot.

"I can always see Camille's work tomorrow."

He shook his head at Mrs. Kathy and headed to the front of the school. He made sure no one was around, then darted out the door in search of King.

∞

Raine ran up the porch and knocked on King's door. Kesha may have had her information wrong. *It has to be a rumor. King can't be that stupid,* he thought.

King's mother opened the door with red eyes. She blew her nose into a piece of tissue. "Hey, Raine."

"I'm looking for King."

She motioned for him to come in.

"Come in," she said, when he didn't move.

Kia burst into tears. Her body shook as she sobbed into her hands. "The Family snatched him out of the yard."

"Why?"

"Something about him robbing their stash house. He was trying to come in the house, but they grabbed him and threw him in a car. He was screaming for me and I couldn't do anything to help him."

Kia laid her head on his shoulder and continued to cry. Raine jumped back from the contact, knocking her head off his shoulder.

"I can't go to the police. You have to save my baby. You know he would do the same for you. King always looked out for you, giving you food."

Raine dropped his head. Whether he wanted to admit it or not, she was right. King did look out for him, many times. He would even risk getting in trouble with her to sneak him food. Still, Raine didn't like being called out by her. Until now, he didn't know she knew about King giving him food. Raine didn't want to do a thing for her but his friend was in trouble. He knew he couldn't leave his friend hanging. He had no choice. He cracked his knuckles and headed out the door.

Raine walked across the street to his house. He slammed his bedroom door and paced around. *Go up against The Family? How could I?* Sure, there had been people that tried but they weren't heard from again. He was only thirteen, but Kia was right. King gave him food when his mother was too high to care.

His heart raced, and his hands were sweaty. He sat under the window and tried to think of another way to help King. *Maybe the police will listen? What if The Family only wants to talk to King?* he thought.

Raine closed his eyes but images of King getting beat up flashed through his mind. He got up from the floor, slid his closet door open and grabbed his metal bat. Raine tightened his hand around the bat, then swung it around a few times. He stormed out of his house with the bat resting on his shoulder.

Raine walked into the daiquiri shop and marched past the counter.

"You can't go back there!"

He ignored the cashier and continued to the back of the shop. He took the bat and banged it against the wall. The sound echoed through the room. The impact combined with his sweaty palms almost caused the metal bat to slip from his grasp, but Raine continued to bang until guys appeared from the back.

"Do we have a problem?" asked one, showing the gun on his waist.

"Where's my friend? Y'all took him."

"Who? We take lots of people."

"King Brooks," said Raine.

The guy rubbed his chin then held up a finger like a light bulb went off. He laughed. "Show him where to find his friend."

The same two guys that jumped him before, handed him another beat down. Raine managed to swing the bat a few times but missed each time. Finally, he curled up and tried to block their punches. Tears threatened to fall but he bit his tongue to keep them at bay.

"That's enough." Dolla walked through the crowd. "We keep meeting like this."

Someone pushed King in front of Dolla. He was a bloody mess. His eyes were swollen shut.

Raine stumbled to King and pulled him to his side. "Let's go, King."

"Not so fast. Your friend here robbed my stash and caused the police to snoop around. I had to move houses. Which has cost money. Your friend isn't going anywhere but to his grave."

Raine looked back at King with teary eyes. He could feel his heart thump and hear King's short, wheezy breaths. The gun was pointed right a King's face. Raine closed his eyes and took a deep breath, wishing when he opened them, he woke up on the floor in his bedroom. He opened his eyes as muffled voices returned to normal. King had managed to open one of his eyes a little. His eyes glistened with tears, but the look was familiar. King wanted him to look out for him, return the favor. Raine knew there was only one way to save King.

He jumped in front of King with his hands raised.

"Wait! We'll get your money back," said Raine.

"How?"

"I'll find a way," said Raine.

Dolla frowned. "Not good enough."

"I'll find a job."

"Get these clowns out my face."

Raine heard a gun click. "I'll get down."

CHAPTER 5

Raine skipped school the next day. He was too sore to go and was afraid the teachers would notice the bruises. After agreeing to join The Family, he was told, well, ordered to meet at the shop the following night. Now, he was sitting in the shop bouncing his leg while he waited for Dolla. Raine planned on being there for a few minutes, an hour at the most, then making up an excuse to leave. He had spent all that time surviving by rummaging for food and by avoiding gangs. King ended that with one stupid decision.

Dolla motioned for Raine. "Say, youngin', come on." Everyone in the shop stopped and spoke to Dolla or gave him dap.

"This is your crew. Crew, this is Raine."

Raine looked around the room and saw the guys that jumped him. He tightened his fists and headed in their direction.

Dolla stuck his arm out. "Don't take the fight to heart. It's the only way we separate the strong from the weak."

"I'm Dizzy. You held your own." Raine gave him dap. He was the one with the scar above his lip.

"This is TJ," said Dizzy.

TJ didn't give Raine dap. He curled up his lip and played with his diamond earring. He was wearing another football jersey, this time it was the Falcons.

"You take orders from Dizzy. Dizzy takes orders from me. Disobey Dizzy, you disobey me. Do I need to remind you about the consequences?" asked Dolla.

Raine shook his head.

"I'm out," said Dolla.

"We need to send a message," said Dizzy. He pulled a piece of paper from his pocket with an address on it.

"A message?" asked Raine.

Dizzy held up his fist to Raine. "A *message*."

Raine didn't care what he promised Dolla. He didn't go around beating on folks because he was ordered. The person did nothing to him. Raine knew he had to think of a way to get out the job.

Dizzy tossed him a black hoodie. "Let's go."

Barely any cars were on the road. The air was cool. The moon was the brightest thing in the sky. Raine thought of ways to reproduce the mood on paper. He was also thinking about taking off running down a dark alley but wondered if he was fast enough to lose them.

"Right here," said TJ.

Raine slapped his head. He took too long to

decide.

"Alright. TJ you go around the back. Raine you go across the street and if anyone comes out stop them."

Raine headed to hide across the street. Dizzy's plan was perfect. He planned on disappearing into the darkness while they waited. Dizzy yelled for him to come back.

"Take the back with TJ."

"What…Why?"

"Dolla told us to look out for you. I don't need you getting hurt on your first job," said Dizzy.

Raine pulled at the neck of the hoodie and tugged on the hem. There was no way he could slip away with TJ near.

Dizzy slapped his hand down. "Stop pulling at your hoodie. You ready or not?"

Raine looked at the house. "Yeah."

"Good. Go to the back," said Dizzy.

Raine walked to the back of the house. He passed by a window and heard jazz music playing in the room. He crouched behind a bush as Dizzy's knocks echoed through the streets, stopping the music.

"Who is that knocking on…"

Raine listened as furniture and glass fell. His heart raced as the footsteps got closer. The backdoor swung open and a man limped out, wheezing.

TJ ran from the bush and tripped the guy. "He's back here!"

"Hold him," said Dizzy.

Raine appeared from the bushes and stood over the guy. TJ had a lock on his arms while Dizzy pointed a gun at him. The guy's eyes were wide as he begged for more time.

Raine put his hand on the gun. "You said we had to deliver a message. How can a dead man receive a message?"

Dizzy pushed him off and lowered the gun. "Dolla said to give you this message."

Dizzy punched the man in the stomach causing him to drop to the ground. They kicked and punched him until he was barely conscious.

"Come get a few licks," said Dizzy.

"Na, I'm good." Raine had taken a seat on the steps and turned his attention to the moon.

Dizzy rushed over and snatched him up. "You punch him, or I'll punch you."

Raine reached back—Dizzy pulled his gun. "You better think about it. Is this crackhead worth your life?"

With the gun pointed to his forehead, Raine relaxed his fist then walked over to the guy. He wondered if all of this was worth it. King was relaxing and healing at home while he was thrown into his worst nightmare.

Raine looked the guy in the eye that wasn't swollen. The man nodded. Raine reached back and delivered a blow to his stomach.

"Again," said Dizzy.

Raine repeated the motion each time Dizzy demanded it.

"Ok. I think he gets the message," said Dizzy.

Raine wiped sweat from his knuckles onto his shorts. Every blow thumped through his body. He tried to walk away but vomit rushed from his mouth.

"Come on, man." TJ lunged for Raine. "You threw up on my jersey."

Dizzy pushed TJ back. "Calm down. You got over a hundred football jerseys."

Dizzy patted Raine on the back. "First time is always the hardest."

Raine stumbled out the yard. His vision blurred as they neared the street.

"Man, I knew this was a bad idea. He's too young for this," said TJ. His voice sounded like he was under water.

Dizzy grabbed Raine and held on to him. "Relax. Slow breaths."

Raine awoke at the back of the shop. He looked around for Dizzy and TJ.

"You passed out." Dizzy handed him a bottle of water and food.

Raine snatched the food from his hands. "Thanks."

"You can go home. I'll hit you up later." He threw Raine a cell phone. Raine eyed the phone, turning it in his hands.

Dizzy reached over and turned on the phone. "Act like you don't know how to work this."

"I don't," said Raine. "Never had one."

∞

The next day, Raine was at school but found that his mind kept wandering to last night. He wasn't listening to any of his teachers and was surprised to find himself at lunch. The day had been a blur. He didn't have lunch since King was still healing. Art always made his hunger pains disappear, so he headed to the art room and saw that the room was dark. He decided to sneak a peek before Mrs. Kathy returned. Raine clicked on the light and headed to the easel.

"Hello, stranger." Mrs. Kathy smiled when he jumped.

"Beautiful, yes?" She walked next to Raine and rubbed his back. "You should have seen her in action."

"I can only imagine."

"You were excited to see her. Is she not your favorite artist?"

Raine nodded.

"Help me understand your absence." She raised her hands, jewelry dangling making its own music.

He shrugged. "Something came up."

"And that something was more important than Camille?"

"I guess so." He pulled his book sack off the floor and headed for the door.

Mrs. Kathy grabbed his arm. "I hope the rumors are not true."

"What rumor?" asked Raine.

He had been with The Family for only a few

days. She couldn't have known.

"Do I need to repeat it?"

Raine dropped his head and tugged at his shorts.

She grabbed his chin and raised it. "That is beneath you. You have far too much talent."

She gave him a bag of food. "You know, Raine, you are loyal to a fault. Not everyone deserves your protection."

"Thanks for the food."

She nodded. "Stay as long as you would like. I hope to see you next period."

Mrs. Kathy began adjusting the classroom while Raine grabbed a seat and sketched in front of Camille's painting. He tried to imitate her continuous lines while avoiding mistakes so that his sketch was clean like Camille's final work and before he knew it the bell rang ending lunch.

The bell rang ending lunch. Raine took his seat as the class began filing in.

"Raine, slide that chair next to you," said Mrs. Kathy.

Raine put the empty chair next to him and prepared his supplies.

"I see you finally got your schedule changed. Take that seat next to Raine. He can help you with anything you need."

Raine glanced back to see who Mrs. Kathy was talking to and frowned.

Mrs. Kathy cleared her throat. "Now, Raine."

Raine huffed and tossed his pencil down. He

couldn't believe his luck. Laila was sitting next to him in two classes now. She was close enough to see the stains on his clothes. He got the art supplies and tossed it in front of her, spilling it.

Laila glanced down at the spilled supplies then to him. "I know you're gonna pick that up."

Raine stared her down. The same way he did dudes that thought he was scary.

Laila snaked her neck. "Pick it up." She reached over and snatched his supplies from his grasp. "I'll just use yours."

Raine looked at his empty hands; clearly, she didn't know about him. Laila pushed the pencils out of his reach when he tried to take them back.

"Give my stuff back." He did his best to intimidate her.

"What are we working on?" asked Laila, ignoring his mean mug.

Raine sighed. "Portraits of a family member."

He used his elbow to cover his sketch when Laila glanced at his paper.

"I didn't wanna see anyway," she mumbled.

"Good."

Raine erased the face he was sketching until he tore a hole in the paper. He didn't know whether to draw the face he remembered as a child or the face that now walked the hall at night. Raine balled up the sketch and grabbed another sheet. He looked over at Laila's paper.

"Who are you drawing? Mrs. Potato Head?" he asked.

Laila punched him on the arm and moved to the

other side of the room. He laughed at her reaction.

A message chimed on his phone.

Dizzy: Tomorrow night at 10

Raine's smile dropped as the all too familiar feeling of fear rushed to his stomach.

∞

Raine finished brushing his teeth. He splashed water on his face before heading down the hall, tapping lightly on his mother's door.

"Ma?"

She was lying on the bed with her eyes wide. Drool fell down the side of her face. Raine watched her body, waiting to see her chest rise.

He tapped her arm. "Latisha?"

He clenched the paper in his hand and waited for her response.

"I need you to sign this lunch form, so I can get free lunch. I would do it, but I don't know my social security number."

She mumbled and flipped over, knocking the silver tray from the nightstand. The white powder danced to the floor.

"What are you doing in here?" yelled Jackson.

His eyes dashed from Raine to his mother and then to the tray on the floor.

He rushed over to Raine and grabbed his collar. "You knocked down my stuff?"

"No!"

"You know how much this stuff cost?"

His eyes were red. Jackson was so close to his face, Raine saw dried powder under his nose.

"Let me go." He tried to snatch away but Jackson only tightened his grip.

"You're gonna pay for that."

He searched Raine's shorts and didn't find anything. He opened his jacket and pulled out his leather sketchbook. Raine tried snatching it back, but Jackson held his hand out to block him. Jackson flipped through the pages and stopped on an image.

"You think this is funny?"

Jackson had flipped to a drawing of himself. Raine drew him sitting on the floor getting ready to inject drugs. He drew sweat dripping from his forehead with ashy, cracked lips. The words on the bottom read: *It be calling me man.*

"I said do you think this is funny?"

Raine looked at the page he was holding up. He remembered walking through the door and finding Jackson on the floor in a panic to get high. He thought about a crack addict named Pookie from the movie *New Jack City*. Raine laughed the whole time he drew the piece. His body screamed for him to remain quiet or make up an excuse for his drawing, but his mind screamed for him to rebel. Although he tried to avoid Jackson, he could not pass up the chance to mess with him.

Raine smirked. "Yeah, Pookie, it's funny."

"Pookie? Okay. I'll show you Pookie."

Jackson punched him in the stomach, face and back causing Raine to drop to the floor. Jackson ripped the page from his book and tossed the book on the floor. Raine crawled to the book but Jackson picked it up again. He tore out all the drawings and ripped them before leaving.

Raine got off the floor and walked around the room picking up the pieces. None of the images were salvageable. A tear dropped from his eye as he stared at the drawing of his mom. Jackson even ripped the note she wrote to him.

Raine dropped the pieces on the floor and glanced back at his mom. She remained sprawled across the bed. He limped to the bus stop and prepared for another battle with his principal.

∞

Raine walked out of the office and exhaled. The principal stayed on his case about bringing in paperwork. He wanted Raine to bring in a free-lunch form signed, a vaccination record and his mother. Raine couldn't get his mom to pay for utilities and food, those forms would never get signed. He always used the excuse that his mom worked three jobs and was barely free. He knew the principal wouldn't accept the excuse he made forever. Raine had to pretend that he had a headache to hide the bruise from Jackson's fist while the principal threatened to make a home visit.

Raine decided to head to first period early to avoid anyone seeing the bruise. When he walked in, Laila was concentrating on her notebook. She looked up and rolled her eyes.

"Keep rolling your eyes," said Raine. He wasn't happy about seeing her either. Raine sat down and rubbed his temple to relieve his headache. When he looked up, she had turned around and was staring at his bruises. Her frown no longer visible. Her lips were tight, and her eyes sympathetic.

"What," he snapped. Raine knew the look she sported. *Poor Raine*, was on the tip of her tongue, and he didn't need anyone feeling sorry for him.

She did a quick jump in his direction. "Holler at me again. I promise you'll have more bruises to worry about."

She spun around in her seat and continued to highlight notes. Raine was shocked that she was still giving him attitude. Anyone else would have backed off. He decided to ignore Laila. He had enough problems with Jackson, the principal, and The Family. He pulled his sketchbook out of his pocket and sighed. Since Jackson ripped his leather covered sketchbook, he was left with the flimsy one he had snatched out of a dollar store.

∞

Raine walked into the shop and joined Dizzy at the pool table. It was 10 at night and although Raine didn't want to be there, he didn't want to be home either. It had been hours since he left school and he was starving. His head ached, and his stomach yearned for food.

"What up, Raine?"

"Nothing much."

Dizzy tried to hand him $300. "Here. This is for the other night."

"I don't want it. Add it to my debt."

"Dolla already got his cut. We were paid $800."

Raine frowned. "$800 for beating up some old man?"

Raine couldn't forget the image of the man's battered body lying on the ground. He wondered if the guy was okay.

Dizzy shrugged. "An old man that reneged on his word."

Raine stomach growled as he looked at the money. He stuck his palm out and Dizzy slapped it in his hand.

"Cool. I'm about to head outside and watch the car show. Are you coming?"

"No, I'm going to find some food," said Raine.

"Go up front, may not be soul food but the shop has a few options," said Dizzy.

Raine treaded to the front and went to order. "What kind of food do you serve?"

The cashier smiled. "Hey, Raine. We have nachos, hot dogs, and some hot crawfish."

He handed her the money. "Let me get two hot dogs and a pound of crawfish."

"The Family eats free. You can take a seat. I'll bring it to you."

Raine thanked her and was about to walk away. "How did you know my name?"

She turned back. "It's my job to know all the members."

Raine found a seat in the back of the restaurant and scoffed down his food after it arrived. *Eats free* continued to echo through his head. He still had the old man on his mind but the more he ate the easier it became.

Although being in a gang was the last thing he wanted for himself, access to hot food was something he liked. Before leaving, he ordered food for his mother. He was anxious to get home and give it to her. He didn't know the last time she had hot food.

The eerie silence greeted him at the door. Still, Raine walked through his house in search of his mother. He walked to his mother's room and found her mattress overturned. He walked into the kitchen with the bag of food swinging next to his leg. He placed the bag on the counter and went to his room. He threw his book sack into the closet and snatched his blanket out. After making a pallet on the floor, he laid on his back and stared at the ceiling.

She always disappeared for hours but nighttime was the hardest. He turned on his side and stared at the sky. She wanted to be out late at night, so why should he care? He was sure that she wasn't thinking about him.

"Ugh!" He jumped off the floor, grabbed his book sack and headed to find his mother.

Some of the streetlights worked, and some didn't. He quickened his pace and tried to walk on well-lit streets. A path he perfected as an eight-year-old afraid of the dark streets, but more afraid of being alone in an empty house. He clenched his book sack strap tighter, scanning his surroundings every few steps.

It took him five minutes to get to the crack house his mother frequented because it was the closest one to their home.

"Latisha," said Dennis. He visited their home regularly for his mother. Dennis didn't have to yell because the house didn't have a door or windows.

Raine waited by the steps while Dennis dragged his fragile frame into the house to get his mother. He came back with her slouched over his shoulder.

"Heeey, Rainbow," slurred Latisha.

Raine grabbed her from Dennis and headed down the street. After a few blocks, Raine had beads of sweat on his forehead.

He paused and tapped her cheek. "You need to wake up and walk. You're dropping all your weight on me."

Raine sat her on the ground and paced around trying to slow his breathing. Latisha leaned over and laid flat onto the ground. He pulled her up and back to her feet but they both fell.

"You need help with her?"

Raine looked back and saw a guy eyeing his mother. Maybe his intentions were to help, but he made Raine uneasy.

"No," Raine replied.

"Are you sure?"

Raine walked toward him. "You got five seconds to get away from us."

Raine snatched Latisha off the ground and dragged her away, not waiting for the guy to respond.

When he made it home, he fixed Latisha's

mattress and laid her down. He got her food and went back to feed her.

"Sit up so I can feed you. Latisha, get up," he yelled when she continued to sleep.

"No, I can't leave her. Mama, are you okay? Wake up, please," she mumbled. A tear slid down her face.

Raine wiped her face and watched her squirm in her sleep. His mother's words left him wondering about his grandma and what happened to her.

∞

It had been a week since King's beating, so Raine headed to King's house before school to check on his recovery. He knocked on the door and waited for an answer.

Kia snatched the door open. "What?"

"I came to check on King."

Kia rolled her eyes. "Hold on. King!"

"What, Ma!"

"Don't what me, boy. Raine's here."

When King neared her, Kia tried to whisper, "Don't let nobody in my house."

Raine walked away from the door heated. Now, he was *nobody* but the other day she invited him inside and pleaded for his help. Raine paced as he tried to calm down before King came outside.

King walked outside pulling a shirt over his head. He had a sling on his left arm and a black eye.

King glanced at the door. "Sickening." He dapped Raine. "What's up?"

"You good?"

"I'm straight. I come back to school next week."

"Oh."

"A dude name Dizzy came and brought me a phone. He said I needed to keep it charged and with me all the time."

Raine nodded. "I know. I have one in my pocket. I have to charge it at school."

"You wanna go somewhere and chill?"

"I just came by to check on you. I'm headed to school."

"Ok. I'll catch you Monday," said King. "You need food?"

"I'm good. Thanks for looking out."

∞

For the first time in a while, Raine stood in the lunch line with money to pay for his food. A few girls chatted behind him about plans for the weekend and a few guys in front tried their best to flirt with girls passing by. Raine sighed wishing the line moved faster, not because of hunger but because he wasn't in the mood. The weight of the money in his hand caused his shoulders to slouch.

The smell of red beans and cornbread made his mouth water. He had an appetite until he grabbed the money from his book sack. For some reason, the old man on the money reminded him of the old man he beat. Then, images of the man's swollen eyes and defeated posture filled his empty stomach with guilt.

He is a crackhead who didn't pay on time. Why should I care? Crackheads chose their path, right? They are selfish and undeserving of sympathy.

"Um, move up."

There was a large hole in the line since he spaced out and didn't move up. He tucked the money into his pocket and slipped out the line. Feeling like the room was closing in on him, he headed outside for fresh air.

He diverted to a nearby table when he spotted Laila at his favorite table. She had the nerve to have her *little* friends with her. Raine kicked a juice carton then sat at the table across from her. He pulled out his sketchbook and twisted a dread. The wind blew his book to a blank page.

He started off with a male figure, like the guy. He was burly with large cheeks. Then the guy's baldhead was replaced with untamed hair and a feminine face. He erased the heavy frame and replaced it with one so fragile that a quick shake of the page would cause her to crumble. After a while, the three attackers were attacking a woman that resembled his mother.

No longer able to look at the picture, he slammed the book closed and tossed his pencil on the table. He looked up in time to catch Laila staring at him. She ignored her friends as they gossiped around her. She looked away when he noticed her.

What was she staring at? Probably the stains on his clothing or his hair in desperate need of a fade. After all, the girls she hung with were all about brand name clothing. Laila did have a designer book sack and new braids since the other day, not that he was paying any attention to her.

He glanced back and watched as she tried to look his way without her friends noticing. Raine kept his eyes trained on her. She kept her eyes on him, calling his bluff. A raindrop fell on his arm, cooling his skin. Rainy days were calmest for him.

Raine laid his head on the table and closed his eyes, relaxing more with every raindrop that fell on his skin. He stayed that way until he heard Laila telling her *new* friends *bye*. He left the table and made his way over to her. Laila rolled her eyes and moved her book sack.

Raine huffed. "You don't have to move your high ass book sack. I didn't wanna touch it anyway."

He was tired of being treated like his skin would damage their precious clothes or make their bodies dirty.

"I was moving my book sack for you to sit down." Laila shook her head and grabbed her things. "Mrs. Kathy said you were one of the sweetest people in this school. I don't know what she sees." She stood and stormed inside the school.

After the bell rang, Raine walked a few paces back from Laila. He continued to the art room while she was pulled to the side by Lewis. His gold chain with his basketball number, thirty-three, dangled over his neck when he leaned down to hug her. Raine mugged them. If she could be friends with someone like Lewis, then he didn't regret talking to her the way he did.

Beads of water slid down the window outside of art class. The class was unusually quiet. The rain not only calmed him but his classmates also. Low thunder and flashes of lightning mixed with the sound of brush strokes and the smell of fresh paint.

Laila was next to him drawing the lopsided portrait of a beautiful woman. Her drawing looked nothing like the woman on the reference picture. He stood by his comment of her drawing looking like Mrs. Potato Head but refrained from mentioning it to avoid another punch. The lady in the picture had a slim face but Laila made it round. *The markings of an amateur*, he thought.

Laila's perfume blended with the smell of paint, occasionally invading his nose. She was friends with Lewis and Essence, and she couldn't draw to save her life. Not to mention she had a smart mouth and a weird accent. He glanced at her concentrating on the horrible drawing and sighed. He owed her an apology. He didn't want to make Mrs. Kathy look bad. *Yeah, that's the reason*, he thought.

Raine dropped his pencil and turned to her. "Look, I'm sorr–"

"Students, I have a surprise guest. This is Mr. Rod. He is a local painter and has come to talk to you all while he paints," said Mrs. Kathy.

Raine spun around and saw the man dressed in modest clothes. Dark grey pants and a black shirt. *A painter's uniform*, he thought.

The man sat at the blank easel and sprayed it with water before beginning. "Like Kathy said, my name is Rod short for Roddy. Don't ask where my mother got the name. I was once a student like you. I grew up a few blocks from Garvey High. I dropped out of school and started on a path to self-destruction…"

Raine listened intently to his words and watched his watercolor technique. A new weapon to add to his arsenal. The man told them how he became a drug addict first, then homeless with no will. He claimed that art was the only thing that pulled him away from death. He went from a drug addict to a well-known local painter, then gained national headlines with his triumphant story and artwork.

After the demonstration, Mrs. Kathy called Raine over to meet Mr. Rod.

"Ah, the famous Raine Landry. Nice to finally put a face to all of the artwork in my email," he held his hand out for Raine to shake.

Raine lightly shook his hand. He grabbed Raine's hand and squeezed it. "Always give a firm handshake. Confidence is key even when you aren't."

Raine nodded.

"Well, I'll let you gentleman converse," said Mrs. Kathy.

"I'm looking for two students from this school to mentor. I want you to be one of them."

"Ok. I'm cool with that."

"Great. You can expect one on one sessions here at school. You will attend gallery openings and meet artists."

"Ok."

"I will also check on your grades and visit you at home regularly."

Raine froze. Everything was great until he mentioned home visits. One step into his house and Mr. Rod would know something was wrong. *Maybe I can make him stay outside or come up with excuses like I did with the principal?*

"So, what do you say?" asked Mr. Rod.

∞

Maybe it was the man's words or the light stream of rain that made Raine get off the bus and head straight to this house. He knocked on the door after wiping water from his face. Raine saw the curtain move but the door remained closed. He knocked again.

"I paid my debt," said a voice from behind the door.

"I'm not here for money," Raine answered.

"What do you want, boy?"

Raine dropped his head. He asked himself that question on the way over. He still didn't know what led him to this guy's house.

"I don't know," said Raine.

A few seconds went by and the man kept his door closed. Raine turned back and headed down the porch. He heard the locks click and the door opened.

"Come on."

Raine dashed up the steps and into his house.

"Leave your wet stuff here. Take those shoes off too."

Raine did as told. He followed the man into the living room. Gold and brass saxophones hung neatly on the wall and a few stood under the mantle. Raine the followed him into the kitchen. The man grabbed a tea kettle off the stove then sat at a table under a broken window. The table rocked when the man sat down.

"Tea?"

"No," said Raine, as his eyes roamed around the kitchen. A few pieces of broken furniture lay by the back door.

"It'll warm you up good," said the guy. He was stocky, not fragile like his mother. Passing him in the streets would give no sign of his addiction.

Raine took the cup from him.

"If you came to apologize, save it," said the guy.

"You play the saxophone?" asked Raine.

"Played. I don't anymore." He inhaled a shaky breath and frowned, grabbing his chest, and rubbing it.

"Why don't you play anymore?" Raine asked.

"What's it to you?"

Raine shrugged. "Don't know. Just wondering."

The man sipped his tea. "Punctured lung. I can barely breathe enough to survive let alone blow on some sax." He waved his thick hands.

"I'm sorry. I didn't mean to."

"You didn't. Got into an argument with a band member and he stabbed me. Ten years ago. I can see in your eyes, boy. You're not like the other two."

"Why are you smoking that stuff?" asked Raine.

He sipped the tea and was surprised that he liked it.

"It's how I deal with life."

"Crackheads are all the same. Take the easy way out because life gets hard. Your problems won't go away."

"Young punk. You don't know me!"

"No, but I know crackheads."

The guy jumped up from the table and tried to rush over to Raine. He stopped short, wheezing. He leaned on the counter and dropped to his knees. His brown lips turning purple.

Raine grabbed his arm and helped him to the couch. He wheezed for a few more minutes then settled. Raine walked around his living room looking at his pictures.

"Is that Anita Baker?"

The man snorted. "What do you know about Anita Baker?"

"My teacher. She plays her music all the time while we paint. Makes my art come spilling out."

"That was in '91. We toured around the world. That's a picture in Africa."

Raine glanced back at the man then at the picture. He had a saxophone in his hand but what caught Raine's eyes was the high top he sported. "You had a high top?"

"Um-hmm. Like your hair now. Except you got those Cheetos looking crap on top."

Raine twisted his hair. "These are dreadlocks, old man."

The man struggled to his feet. He pointed to a picture. "That's not dreadlocks. This is dreadlocks."

Raine got butterflies in his stomach. "You knew Bob Marley!"

"Knew him. I beat him in soccer one time." He laughed and took a seat again.

Raine pulled out his sketchbook and showed him a pencil drawing of Bob Marley.

"You did this? Looks like a picture." The guy ran his hand over the drawing.

Raine sat on the couch next to him. Silence reclaimed the room.

"I came because I couldn't get you out of my head. I got paid for beating you up, you know?" He tried to give the man the money. "Here, I don't want it."

"I don't want your money. Shouldn't you be getting home? I know your mama's worried."

Raine, angry that he didn't take the money, stood and headed to the door. "Trust me. She doesn't give a damn about me. Thanks for the tea."

His mother was the source of his problems. She was the reason he had to turn down Mr. Rod's mentor offer.

The man nodded. "Lock the door on your way out. I didn't get your name."

"I didn't give it to you." Raine opened the door and headed out. He could see that the storm was worse. Instead of walking down the steps, he felt pulled by the old man's spirit.

Raine sighed and turned back. "My name is Raine."

"Appropriate name for today's weather. The name's Al."

CHAPTER 6

Raine headed to the bathroom after first period. He was trying to maneuver through the crowd of students changing classes. Accidentally bumping someone could lead to a suspension. A turned-up lip or frown like he stunk would mean a quick right to the jaw. He ignored the girls because they usually screeched and ran off.

The seniors thought it was funny to run and push everyone forward causing them to become jammed, resulting in a few falls. Screams and laughter filled the hallway. Raine managed to get out the hallway but tripped over the threshold. The front of his shoe ripped open.

"Look at Raine, his shoes talking," Essence said, pointing at him.

Essence, Lewis, and their crew laughed. Laila on the other hand kept a straight face and remained quiet. She dropped her head when their eyes connected.

"You lucky I don't hit girls. You have a brother?" Raine asked.

"I sure do," said Essence.

"Where is he, so I can beat him up?"

Essence rolled her eyes and popped her shiny lips. "He's in pre-school, stupid."

"I'll still kick his ass," said Raine.

Laila giggled but stopped when Essence and the crew looked at her. Essence waved him off and walked away. They all followed her like a bunch of robots, Laila included.

It was only a matter of time before Laila acted like them, he thought. She hung with them and dressed like them. He was sure they filled her in on his status as the dirty kid with a crackhead mother.

Raine walked off, trying to avoid ripping his shoes more. When he was down the hall, he pulled the shoe off. The glob of dried glue no longer held his shoe together. He headed to art class to glue the layers again.

"I don't know why you won't let me buy you more shoes," Mrs. Kathy said. She plugged in the hot glue gun then handed it to him.

"I'm good," said Raine.

He didn't like being in debt to anyone. He already had to put his life on hold to repay Dolla. There was no way he would fall for that again. Besides, he had money. He would buy new shoes when the time came. For now, hot glue was enough.

∞

Raine jumped awake when he heard choking. Dazed, he glanced around the dark room, mad that his sleep was interrupted again. A loud crash made him jump so hard his body trembled. He jumped to his feet and rushed toward the noise. He eased the squeaky bathroom door open.

"Ma!"

She was sprawled across the floor with white foam coming from her mouth and her body jerked. Jackson was standing near her with glossy eyes. He looked up at Raine with his mouth and eyes wide open.

Raine rushed to her side and continued to yell her name. Her eyes rolled to the back of her head. Raine turned to Jackson with tears rolling down his face.

"Help." His voice broke and the words came out hoarse, needy, and desperate.

Jackson backed out of the bathroom and down the hall. Soon after, Raine heard the front door open and close. He grabbed his mother into his arms and rocked her, while begging for her to wake up.

He tried to think of anyone that would help, but no one came to mind besides King. He laid his mother down and rushed out the door. The rocky pavement didn't slow down his bare feet as he zoomed across the road. He knocked on King's door until he realized no one was coming to the door. He ran back to his house and back to his mother's side. She was still unconscious, but the jerking had stopped. Then he remembered the cellphone Dizzy gave him. He ran and grabbed it. His hands trembled as he pressed the numbers.

"9-1-1, what's your…"

Raine hung up the phone. He couldn't call the ambulance. They would have to come inside to get his mother. He glanced back; his mother was seizing again. The phone vibrated in his hand. The operator was calling back. He ran his hands over his face. If he answered the emergency responders would have to come in. He knew with one glance inside his house, he would be hauled away, but if he didn't answer his mother would die.

"Hello."

"This is the emergency operator. I'm returning a hang up from this number. Do you need help?"

"Ah, no. I don't but there's a woman on the ground shaking."

"Where are you?"

Raine read off the address. "She's laying on the sidewalk outside a burgundy house."

"Who am I speaking with?"

Raine hung up. He struggled to get his mother out of the house. By the time he got to the porch, he was covered in sweat. He gently laid her outside their neighbor's house. He placed his hand on her stomach, waiting for it to rise and fall. Her body remained still.

He paced and ran his hand through his hair. Tears streamed down his face. Raine held her until he heard the ambulance in the distance. He kissed her cheek and ran back into the house, hiding in the living room and watching out the window to get a better view.

The paramedics ran over to his mother.

"Another overdose," one yelled.

Soon after, two police cars showed up. The paramedic pointed to the spot they found her. The police walked to Raine's neighbor's door. Raine knew the knocks would go unanswered because the elderly lady never left her home. A nurse would sit with her daily and even ran her errands.

A few people went outside when they heard the sirens. Raine was scared that someone would name his mother and blow his plan. His nerves settled when the police walked back to their cars.

"Hey, did you check this house?" asked the officer.

He was pointing at Raine's house. His stomach sunk, and his heart raced. The officer was shining his flashlight right at the window he was sitting under. Raine slumped down to the floor and watched the light shine through the living room.

"That house must be abandoned. Look at all the grass around it," said the second officer.

"I'll check to make sure."

"Ok. But if a big snake wraps around your legs don't call for backup. I'm not coming. I'll flash a light or siren but I'm not getting out."

Raine heard the officers laugh and then car doors slam. He released a deep breath when he heard them pull away. He listened to the ambulance siren until he couldn't hear it anymore.

∞

Raine sat on the public bus behind a baby that kept turning back and looking at him. The mother had turned him around a couple times, but the baby was set on annoying Raine. The seats were hot and sticky, and the bus driver played the news instead of music. The baby reached his chubby hand out to him, Raine shook his head and looked out the window.

He heard something drop. When he turned back the baby was halfway over the seat reaching out to him and had caused his mother to drop her phone.

"He's not always this friendly. Actually, he isn't friendly at all. I'm Latisha and this is my son, Joshua."

"Raine."

"You want to hold him?" she asked.

He didn't want to hold her baby. Why did she have to share the same name as his mother?

"Um…"

She got up and placed the baby in Raine's arms. He reached up and grabbed the side of Raine's face. He had to admit the baby was cute and he smelled like baby lotion. Before he knew it, the boy was sprawled in his arms because he had rocked him to sleep.

"This is our stop," she said. She took the boy from Raine and grabbed his diaper bag. "Nice to meet you, Raine."

"Same," said Raine.

He was on his way home from visiting two hospitals. The first had no record of his mother and the last said they couldn't give information to a minor. The entire day at school Raine expected someone to pull him out of class and give him bad news.

After getting off the bus, he took a slow walk home. Even though he already had to take care of himself, the thought of her dying never crossed his mind.

He reached his house and walked in. His first stop was his mother's room. Empty.

∞

At school the next day, Mrs. Kathy gave Raine paint and a canvas. She had also tried the whole class period to get him to open up, but he didn't budge. There was no way he would tell anyone about his mother or his night.

"Raine, you coming to the park?" asked King after Raine had gotten off the bus and was heading home.

"No."

Raine planned to drop off his art supplies then head out to the hospitals again. Maybe he would have better luck this time.

He walked into the house and saw his mother sitting on the floor. She was drinking from a water bottle and eating chips. Hospital bands dangled from her wrist. She jumped from the floor and ran over to him, pulling him into a tight hug. Raine closed his eyes to keep his tears at bay. He relaxed in her arms, not wanting to pull away.

She ran her hand through her wild hair and smiled. "Hey, Rainbow."

He walked off to his room and slammed the door. He was relieved but angry. Raine wondered where she got the chips and water. He hated when she would beg in front of the liquor store. She didn't care if she begged adults or his classmates, and how did she find time to beg?

She opened his door. "The nurses chipped in and gave me money for some food. You want me to fix you a sandwich?"

"When did you get here?"

"A little after twelve," she replied. "I got us some food."

"Not hungry."

"Ok."

"They let you leave the hospital this soon?" he asked.

"I discharged myself. You know I don't like hospitals."

Raine shook his head. Figures she would leave the only place that could help her with drug rehab. He turned his back to her and organized his art supplies. He turned back when he heard his room door close. *Yeah, run,* he thought.

After a few sketches, he had his piece planned.

He heard a soft knock on the door. "Hey, I brought you a sandwich. In case you get hungry later."

Raine ignored her as he prepped the paint.

"Are you working on something new? You mind if I watch?"

Raine exhaled and looked at the ceiling. "Why?"

His mother hadn't watched him paint in months. Every blue moon she wouldn't get high for a day or two and pretend like she cared.

She took a seat on the floor. "Go ahead. You won't know I'm here. I wanted to…"

"The school needs you to go fill out my paperwork and I'm behind on shots."

"I'll go up to the school this week."

Raine relaxed at the first sound of the brush stroke against the canvas. Not even the lie she just spat could take him out of his zone.

∞

The next morning, his first stop was the art room.

"This is…I don't even have words to describe it," said Mrs. Kathy.

She ran her hand over Raine's artwork. "Talented isn't appropriate anymore. You are a prodigy, maybe a genius."

Raine twisted a dreadlock while she marveled at his work. He didn't think the piece was that great. Yesterday, he couldn't put the brush down. He hadn't been that focused in a while. He hated to admit it, but his mother was the reason the inspiration came flowing out. She watched over his shoulder the whole time.

"Are you gonna hang it up?"

"Child, I am going to do a lot more than that."

"There's the bell. I better get to first period." Raine eased out the door and glanced back at Mrs. Kathy. She was so wrapped up in his piece that she didn't see him leave.

Raine heard King's voice before entering the classroom. He gave King a nod. Of course, Laila was in her seat with her notebook open and ready for the lesson. Raine decided to try his luck and speak to her.

"Morning." He smirked when she raised a brow and ignored him.

"Laila, can I get the notes from Friday?" asked a classmate.

"Yeah, let me get the notes too and your phone number," yelled King.

Raine pretended to search through the book as he waited for Laila's response.

"Nope."

The class erupted in laughter.

Someone yelled, "She played you."

King smacked his lips. "I didn't want her number anyway. Lame geek."

"Lame is pretending to be hard when you're not," said Laila.

A few *Oh's* came from the class.

"Stop playing with me you lil' nappy headed, black…"

Raine stood in the way as King made his way to Laila.

"Be cool, King."

King snatched away from Raine. "She better watch who she's talking to."

Laila stood behind Raine with her arms folded. "Or what?"

"In your seats." Mr. Riker walked in and began the lesson, interrupting the show they were putting on.

In art class, Laila sat next to him. Class had begun twenty minutes ago, and she hadn't spoken a word. Even though he was doing little things to get a reaction, she continued to ignore him.

"Can I borrow your green?" asked Raine.

Laila shrugged.

"You and your friends need to find another lunch table."

"I sit where I want, Raine."

He almost smiled at the way she said his name. Calm and not bothered by his threat.

"Class, I have an invitation to a community spray paint party. Everyone is invited to attend and contribute a small piece to the wall in 9th ward," said Mrs. Kathy. "The paint supplies will be provided."

She passed out the flyers and stopped by Raine. "I hope to see you there."

∞

Raine received a text from Dizzy for another job. Dizzy's text interrupted a weird conversation with his mother, so he was relieved to be away. Raine had come to expect her promises but like every other time, she would get high and forget about him and her word.

He got to the shop and took a seat on the sofa.

"What's up?" asked Dizzy.

Raine twisted a dread. "You tell me."

"So, look, we have to drop off this package and get the money."

Raine sighed. "Are you sure that's all?"

"Yeah."

Raine pointed to the pool table. "Then what's with the gun?"

"For protection." Dizzy checked his phone. "Where is King?"

TJ walked through the door eating nachos. "Y'all ready?"

"We would be if King was here on time," said Dizzy. He called King's phone and cussed when it went to voicemail.

"First job and he's already messing up. I don't know why Dolla put him on," said Dizzy.

"We're already ten minutes behind," said TJ.

"Raine, call your boy," Dizzy said.

"I don't have his number."

"We out," said Dizzy.

They walked out towards a car and heard gravel crushing under footsteps. Dizzy quickly pointed his gun in that direction.

King ducked and covered his head. "Chill! It's me."

Dizzy dropped the gun. "Are you stupid? Why are you late?"

"My mama had to make a stop."

Dizzy threw his hands up. "You let your mama drop you off? This man is slow." He turned to Raine. "And this is the person you defended? Clowns."

Raine and King got in the backseat.

"Why didn't you come get me?" King whispered.

"I didn't know you was coming. Why didn't you walk?"

"I didn't feel like it," King said.

Raine leaned closer to King and whispered, "Try to stay in the background."

"Ok. We make the drop and get out. If things get hot, y'all better have my back," said Dizzy, as the car rolled to a stop.

He looked at each one and waited until they agreed. "Cool. Let's go."

He gave TJ the duffle bag and extended a gun to Raine.

Raine shook his head. "I'm good. I don't need a gun."

"You have no choice," said Dizzy.

"I said no."

Dizzy grabbed Raine's shirt. "Take the gun or I'll give you something else."

"No."

"Man, we don't have time for this," said TJ.

"Give it to me. I'll carry it," King said.

Raine's eye's darted over to King. *Why would he volunteer to carry the gun?* He just told him to stay in the background.

"No," said Dizzy. "Raine carries it or we go in exposed."

King eyed the gun. "Why can't…"

"You heard what I said," said Dizzy.

They turned to Raine. Their intimidation almost made him extend his hand, but he felt a force, like a magnet pulling him back. He shook his head.

"I guess we're going in without a strap," said

Dizzy. "If anyone gets hurt, Raine will have to face the consequences… and Dolla."

"Let's get this over with," said Raine.

They walked past the guards and through a metal fence. The guard pushed open a door and led them to a man with a cigar in his mouth. He lit it as they walked up. The walls were lined with more guards with guns Raine's height, on their faces were black ski masks. Raine felt like he had walked into a mob movie.

"Dolla recruiting y'all early," said the guy.

TJ dropped the bag on the floor. The guy signaled for one of his men to do the same. TJ grabbed the bag and started walking toward the door.

Dizzy grabbed the bag and unzipped it. "This is twenty-five stacks. You told Dolla thirty-five thousand."

"I told him twenty-five and it's all there. Now, get out."

"You're short ten," said Dizzy.

The guy pulled his gun. "Take that as a late fee and leave."

"Dizzy let's go man," said TJ, as he and King backed towards the exit.

"Nah, he needs to pay me in full."

The guns cocked, sending chills into Raine's body. King and TJ ran out the door. Completely abandoning their promise to Dizzy. Raine knew a thing about broken promises.

"Have some sense like your friends and get ghost," said the guy.

"Pay what you owe," said Dizzy.

"Have it your way."

Raine's hands trembled. He felt sweat dripping down his back. Any second, he would vomit. He exhaled and took a step up to Dizzy.

"I suggest you think about that," Raine said.

The guy laughed. "You're what, ten? I know you have school or something, go home. Don't be dumb like your friend."

Raine pulled out his phone and held it up. "I'm supposed to text the crew four letters after we leave. *DONE.* If I don't, then they'll come in. Do you really want a war with The Family? You run business in Dolla's turf because he allows you to. Do you want to mess that up over ten thousand?"

The guy looked at Raine. "Don't make a difference to me."

"Then do your thing," said Raine. "But be prepared for the consequences." Raine bit his tongue to keep his teeth from clattering.

The guy rotated the rings on his finger. "Go get the ten stacks and get them out of my place."

Raine released a shaky breath. The guy counted ten stacks and placed it in the duffle bag. Raine and Dizzy rushed out the building. When they reached the gate, they ran to the car.

TJ and King were sitting on the curb. They jumped up when Raine and Dizzy ran up.

TJ reached for the bag. "That was crazy, ya heard me."

Dizzy pushed him away and gave the bag to Raine. "What's crazy is you breaking out when the time came to have my back."

TJ walked away and waited by the door. Dizzy eyed King and he did the same.

"Good lookin', Raine," said Dizzy.

On the way back, a sticky silence filled the car and it was suffocating Raine. The silence made the blinkers sound like bass from a rap song. King who was usually mouthing off had his attention on the view outside the window. Raine was still a little shaky from their encounter.

Dolla was waiting for them when they pulled up. He laughed. "Any trouble?"

"Yeah, he tried to short us ten, but Raine and I handled it."

Dolla opened the shop door.

"Wh…what's he doing here?" asked Dizzy.

Dolla walked over to the guy. "This is Tape."

Dizzy walked up to him. "Tape just tried to rob us. Why is he here?"

Dolla pulled him back. "Chill, Dizzy. This is one of my partners."

"How come I've never seen him before? Another test?" asked Dizzy.

Dolla nodded. "A test that two of you failed. Tape here just let me know Dizzy held it down without fear, and Raine, the youngest out of you four, held it down too. TJ and King kick rocks."

TJ and King disappeared through the door. TJ made sure to slam the door on the way out.

"You need to get rid of those two. They folded way too quick," said Tape.

"TJ is family. I promised my uncle I would look

out for him and King owes me," said Dolla.

"I say cut it as a lost and turn the kids loose. I can see in their hearts," said Tape.

"I'll keep an eye on TJ, but King needs to be taught a lesson," said Dolla.

"Hey, your crew your choice. Now, that lil' dude right there didn't buckle. No fear in him."

They looked back at Raine who was sitting on the sofa with his sketchbook. Raine kept his head down and ignored his compliment.

"That's Raine," said Dolla.

"Oh, that's the lil' homie," said Tape. "I see why you want him under your wing. He reminds me of someone."

Dolla laughed. "Whatever, man. I'll hit you up later."

After Tape left, Dolla had Raine and Dizzy recount the stacks of money. He tossed Dizzy two stacks and Raine one stack.

"Put this on my debt," said Raine.

"I already took one thousand. You can take the other," said Dolla.

Raine looked at the stack of twenties, neatly packed like a brick.

"You're giving me a thousand dollars?" asked Raine. "Why?"

Dolla nodded to Dizzy. Dizzy pushed Raine towards the door.

"You are the only person I know that questions everything. Just go with the flow," said Dizzy.

"I would rather put all the money to my debt," said Raine.

"Your debt? You mean King's debt?"

Raine walked out the door. "Mind your business."

"Look at it this way. You'll be paying Dolla until you're fifty if King doesn't help," Dizzy said. "I'll catch you later."

∞

Raine grabbed his book sack and headed for the door. He had a sandwich in one hand and a cold drink in the other. For the first time in months, his mother had stocked the cabinet with food.

"Hey, where are you headed?" asked Latisha.

"Event for school."

"Be safe."

Raine swung the door open. "Now you care?"

"I've always cared, baby."

Raine continued out the door and made sure to slam it. He grabbed his sketch pad and drew a third line under the heading *Mom*.

Raine rode the bus to the lower ninth ward. He walked up at the end of Mrs. Kathy's speech…

"It has been years since Hurricane Katrina, but the city still has scars, empty buildings, rubble, and shattered families. But I would like to think of this day as a step in the right direction. The new housing projects will provide many families with townhomes. The neighborhood looks more like a suburb than a housing project. Now, the new homes reflect the motivation of our kids. They can claim the lower ninth ward with pride. Crime is down, and pride is up. The wall will hold art of our kids. The future of this city. Thanks for coming out and let's get busy."

Raine gave her a quick wave as she left the podium. She was about to be interviewed by the news station. Mrs. Kathy pointed to a blank spot on the wall. She had covered a large square with plastic to reserve it for him. While everyone else had a small square to work on, Raine had a whole side to work on. At times, Raine believed she gave him too much credit. She believed in his talent more than he did.

Raine went to the center and grabbed his supplies, deciding to mix mediums: spray paint and liquid paint. He mixed the paint as Laila walked up next to him with a guy, Raine frowned and mugged the guy.

"Here you go. Make sure to leave enough space for Raine Landry to work," said the guy.

Raine glanced over at Laila. He eyed the pink shade of lip gloss on her lips. Not too much like Essence, Laila applied the perfect amount. Raine turned his lip up when she looked at him.

"Excuse me. That spot is reserved for someone. You're welcome to pick another spot," said the guy, an orange bandana was tied around his neck.

"Reserved for Raine Landry? I'm Raine Landry."

The guys eyes widened. "I was expecting a grown man, honey. Well, carry on." He sashayed back to the entrance.

Raine looked over his shoulder at Laila grabbing a spray paint can. She walked back to the wall and aimed the can at the wall. Raine grabbed her arm and spun the can around.

"You want a pink face? You had the nozzle pointed at your face."

Raine dropped his hand when he realized he was still holding her arm. He wondered why she didn't yank away.

"Thanks," she responded.

Raine tilted his head and moved his shoulders in preparation for art mode. He zoned out as he maneuvered the spray cans. Two hours later, he dropped the can and stepped back to look at his work.

When he turned around a camera flashed in his face causing him to shield his eyes. A crowd had gathered to watch him work. Laila was sitting on the ground right behind him.

"Ladies and gentlemen, I give you Raine Landry," said Mrs. Kathy.

"What do you call this piece?" asked the camera guy.

Raine looked at his art. "Conditional."

"Don't you mean *unconditional*," asked the guy.

Raine frowned. Every time he got a hug from his mama it was conditional. She hugged him after he cut a yard and earned ten dollars, five for her and five for food. She hugged him when he agreed to pawn his bed. She hugged him when he saved her from an overdose.

Raine shook his head. "No."

The picture was of a mother cradling an infant. He made sure to give the baby chubby hands like Joshua.

"Ok. Gather around and get some good pictures of the artwork," said Mrs. Kathy. "Raine, nice work."

Raine began cleaning his mess. When he looked up Laila was gone.

After chatting with Mrs. Kathy, he went to the fast food restaurant down the street. He wanted to order a couple burgers and head home. He ordered and glanced around, spotting Laila at a table in the back.

Raine walked over to the cashier, "Can you change my order. I'm dining in."

He grabbed the food tray and walked over to Laila's table. He dropped the tray down and took a seat.

"Thought I'd return the favor and steal your table."

Laila shrugged and continued eating.

Raine shook the table lightly. "You need to find another table at school."

Laila threw her napkin down. "Why are you so mean to me?"

Raine smirked. For some reason, he enjoyed getting under her skin.

"I'm not," he answered.

"You are mean to me."

"I asked you nicely to leave my table."

She yanked her head back. "I don't think 'shake the spot' is asking me nicely."

Raine laughed. He grabbed a fry from her tray. Laila stood and grabbed a handful of his fries.

Raine looked at her hand and his tray. "Damn,

you took all my fries. I took one of your fries." He held up a finger.

"I don't care. You shouldn't be putting your hands in my stuff."

Laila stuffed the fries in her mouth when he reached for them back. She coughed and reached for her drink.

Raine laughed. "That's what you get."

Laila couldn't talk, so she rolled her eyes and patted her chest. Raine leaned back in his chair and waited for her to finish chewing his fries. He was thinking of something else to do or say to make her angry, so she would wrinkle her nose before fussing at him.

"That wasn't funny. I could've choked to death."

"But you didn't."

"Why did you name your artwork 'conditional'? I think a mother's love is unconditional."

"I don't," he replied.

After a few seconds of silence, Laila asked. "Why are you mean to me?"

"Why did you take over my table?"

"Why do you care about a dumb table?" she sighed. "I sat outside that day because I didn't know where else to sit."

"Where did you move from?" he asked.

"Donaldsonville. All my friends are there. I didn't know anyone here."

"I guess you don't have that problem anymore." Raine nodded towards the door and started grabbing his food.

Essence and the crew were coming in. Lewis made it a point to walk over to Laila.

"What's up, Laila?" Lewis asked, eyeing Raine.

Raine walked to the front counter to order a burger for his mother. He glanced back and saw Essence whispering to Laila. He grabbed his bag as someone bumped into him. Raine turned around and was face to face with Lewis' friend.

"I touched this dirty bum. I need a shower," he said, making Lewis laugh.

Raine tightened his fist. "What was that?"

"You heard me," Lewis' friend said.

Raine knew Lewis had to be running his mouth. He had never seen his friend before, and he was already calling him dirty. Yes, he still had a few drops of paint on his clothes, but so did Laila and they weren't calling her dirty. Raine walked in their direction but was stopped by Laila's arm. He didn't know how she made it to him so fast. He looked down at her and she shook her head.

Raine backed out of her reach. "Keep running your mouth. You can get beat up just like your friend."

"I didn't wanna touch your dirty self," said Lewis.

"Keep telling yourself that, boy," said Raine.

Laila grabbed his arm. "Come on."

"She keeps touching his crusty…" Raine jumped over and punched Lewis in the face. The manager yelled for all of them to leave. Laila dragged Raine out the door and to the bus stop.

He pushed her away. "Why are you always

touching me? Does it look like I want to be touched?"

Laila dropped her hands. "You don't have to worry about me touching you anymore."

She walked away from the bus stop.

"Girl, where are you going?" Raine yelled after her.

She walked to the corner and used her phone. Raine took a seat on the bench and watched her lean against a pole until a car came and picked her up. He had to wait another thirty minutes before the next bus came. He opened his book sack and grabbed the stack of money. He pulled two hundred dollars off the top and stuck it in his pocket.

CHAPTER 7

Raine didn't know the last time he felt this good. He went to the store and for the first-time bought a few items: toothpaste, toothbrush, deodorant, soap, towels, underwear, a new uniform, and shoes. Even the bucket of cold water felt warm.

"Rainbow!"

He turned back to see his mom trying to catch up.

"Stop making all those faces, boy. I'm dressed right." She waved her hands down her body.

Latisha's thin hair was pulled into a tiny ponytail. Her clothes were wrinkle and her sandals were missing the buckle.

Raine raised a brow. "Where are you going?"

"I'm coming to your school to sign those papers."

"For real?"

"Yeah. Let's go before we miss the city bus."

Latisha walked off but stopped when Raine didn't move. Raine had been trying to get her to the school for months.

"Are you coming?" she asked.

Raine pulled out his sketchbook and added a fourth line. He placed the sketchbook in his pocket and followed her.

"Raine, are you coming to school?" yelled King, from the bus stop.

"I'll be there."

Latisha cleared her throat. "You got enough to eat? You know I made groceries."

Raine adjusted his book sack. "How did you get the money?"

She remained quiet.

"I'm getting enough food, thanks."

"You're welcome. Let me see your sketches."

Raine pulled out his sketchbook and gave it to her.

"Let me see the one I gave you. I know you got something good in there."

Raine cleared his throat. "I lost it."

"I know how much you loved that book."

She was the reason his book was ruined. She was the reason Jackson visited and made his life hell.

Raine walked past her. "Whatever. Let's get to the school before you change your mind."

Latisha and Raine waited in the front office for the principal.

He extended his hand. "You are a hard woman to contact," he stated. "Dr. Comeaux; I'm the principal here."

"Latisha Landry, nice to meet you."

"Follow me please."

Latisha tried to smooth down Raine's shirt collar. He moved out of her reach.

"I need you to fill out these forms," said Dr. Comeaux.

Latisha filled out each form and chatted with the principal. Raine wondered if the principal could tell that she was a drug addict. He watched his mom laugh and joke with the principal. Although, she was skinny with shorter hair and black circles around her eyes, watching her smile was like watching her former self. Raine never thought it would be possible for him to get mentored by Mr. Rod, but his mother was doing better each day.

"Ok. That will be all. Just get the doctor to print out his shot record and Raine will be good to go."

"I will do that. Have a nice day."

Raine walked her to the entrance. "Good looking out."

"See you at home."

∞

Raine marked a sixth line in his sketchbook. Latisha was still hanging around the house checking on him every other hour. The other night she came in late and told Raine she did yard work all day to get their power and water back on. Raine didn't believe her until he woke up to his bedroom light on and running water. Although, a few visitors still dropped by unannounced, Jackson hadn't been by in a while. The last thing he needed was a bed.

He knocked on her door. "Ma, are you busy?"

"Reading this book. What's up?"

"You're reading again?"

She smiled. "You see this book in my hand, huh?"

"A delivery truck is on the way. I bought myself a bed and dresser."

Raine held his chin up and smirked. Being in The Family wasn't so bad. He now had food, a new bed on the way, and somehow his mother was looking better each day. He had even convinced the thrift store to sell him furniture.

Latisha closed the book and dropped her head. "Raine?"

"What?"

"Where did you get the money?"

"I saved the money from the drawings I sold." His cellphone vibrated with a text from Dizzy.

"The new cell phone is from art money?"

Raine nodded.

"Ok. I'll be here," she said.

"Cool."

He headed to the daiquiri shop after getting the text from Dizzy. The parking lot was filled with guys revving their car engines. Loud music boomed from the speakers. No one bothered to call the police because of the noise. Dolla had a few dirty cops on his payroll.

"My boy looking fresh. Check you out. About time you get rid of them small shorts and faded shirt. You make me wanna go back to school."

Raine laughed and pushed Dizzy away. "Go head, man."

King and TJ walked in and joined them.

"What's up, Dizzy?" asked TJ.

Dizzy ignored him. TJ walked over to Raine and pulled at his shirt. "About time your project rat looking ass get some new clothes."

Raine pushed him off. Again, TJ grabbed him almost ripping his shirt.

Dizzy walked over and punched TJ in the face. "Leave him be. You heard me?"

TJ grabbed his jaw and mugged Dizzy. He bumped Raine on his way out the shop.

"I bet he's gonna snitch to Dolla," said Dizzy. "Anyway, Dolla want us to chill tonight and enjoy the car show. Everybody from The Fam *must* be here. So, no, Raine, you can't leave."

King rubbed his hands together. "I'm ready to party."

Raine pushed the door open and someone on a motorbike was spinning the back tire. He had to jump back so he wouldn't get hit.

Off to the side of the parking lot was a crowd of members showing off for a camera. The camera man panned through them as they rapped the lyrics to a song and threw up The Family gang symbol. Some had bandanas on, and some had shirts on that had The Family in bold letters. Raine thought the camera man had nerves of steel because some of the members had semi-automatic weapons and they were pointing them at the camera.

"Raine." Dolla waved him over. "This is Raine."

Raine nodded to the group of men.

"This is the youngin' that held it down. How old are you?" asked Tape.

"Thirteen," said Raine.

"TJ's sixteen and been putting in work since he was his age and still haven't learned a thing." Tape staggered over to Raine. "Holla at me if you need anything, Fam."

"Ok."

Tape turned back. "I almost forgot. Here." He took off his chain and placed it around Raine's neck. "Welcome to The Family."

Raine picked up the chain. The diamonds in the name alone had to be a few thousand dollars. Tape extended him some weed. He remembered the first time he found his mother high. He was eight years old. He cried next to her until she came down off her high hours later.

Raine held his breath. "I'm good."

"My bad. You're a drinker," said Tape.

"Go chill with your crew," said Dolla.

Raine was happy he butted in. He didn't want to offend Tape by declining his liquor too. Raine walked to where King and TJ stood. King stared at his chain.

"Where did you get that chain?" asked King.

Raine glanced down. The diamonds from the chain sparkled under the light. "Tape gave it to me."

"Are we getting chains?" asked King.

"How should I know?" Raine said.

Throughout the party, Dolla called Raine over

and introduced him to his *associates*. Each had a piece of knowledge to pass to him. Raine battled with accepting advice about life from drug dealers. *They're bad people, right?* If he hadn't known about their lifestyles, they would've passed for motivational speakers, like the ones that visited his school.

∞

Raine added a seventh line to his sketchbook. He shoved the book into his pocket and jogged to catch up with Laila.

"How long are you going to ignore me?" he asked, grabbing her arm.

She moved away. "We don't touch each other, remember?"

"Look…"

"Leave me alone." She walked into the class and he followed.

She pulled out her notes, displaying her neat handwriting and bright highlighter. She placed headphones on and ignored him for the rest of class. She rushed out of first period to avoid him. Raine decided to hang back until lunch to catch her.

The bell rang to dismiss third period, and Raine rushed to catch up with Laila.

"Raine, I have something for you," said Mrs. Kathy, maneuvering through the students packed in the hallway. She clapped her hands at a couple leaning on the lockers. "Stop that kissing."

Raine watched Laila walk farther down the hall. "Can it wait?"

"If you don't want to see your picture on the front page of the paper, then I guess it can wait."

"I'm in the newspaper?"

Mrs. Kathy held up the paper. He read over the write up. The reporter was praising his work and calling him a prodigy of Mrs. Kathy's and comparing his work to Camille's.

"Go ahead and keep it. I have plenty more copies."

"Thanks."

Raine hadn't looked up from the paper since grabbing it. He continued to read and walk towards the lunchroom. He bumped into a few people, but the paper still had his attention.

"That smile looks nice on you," said Mrs. Kathy.

Raine searched the cafeteria for Laila. He looked over the lunchroom and couldn't find her. He got in line and was able to get lunch for free because Latisha had pulled through. He headed outside to his favorite table and saw her.

He placed his lunch on the table. "Why are you eating at my table?"

He pulled the newspaper from his book sack when she ignored him.

"Look."

He opened the paper and put it in her face after she refused to look his way. He watched her eyes scan the article.

"I'm happy for you." Sadness dripped from her

voice making his stomach twist.

"I wanted to apologize for…"

"Ay, Raine. Here."

Raine frowned when he heard King's loud voice. King tossed him a brown bag.

"I'm good," said Raine.

"You don't need food?"

Raine glanced at Laila. "No. My mama signed my paperwork. I get free lunch now."

King laughed. "Stop lying."

Raine snapped his head to King. "What's funny?"

King always passed him lunch on the side. Never in front of anyone and he hadn't offered him food since they started working with The Family.

"What's funny," Raine repeated.

King threw his hands up. "I see you in your feelings. I'm out."

Raine went to another table and ate his food. When Laila glanced his way, he pretended to concentrate on his lunch. Now, she knew he had a drug addicted mom and needed food from King.

∞

Raine had wracked his brain trying to think of a way to get Laila to talk to him. No one, other than King, took the time to get to know him. He was always looked at as the poor, dirty outcast. No girls would look his way unless it was to call him dirty or call his hair nappy. Most of the kids in his neighborhood were low income families but there was a clear distinction of the poorest kids. Even though everyone wore uniforms, students still knew who were better off. Raine's uniform and yellowish sneakers gave him away.

Raine marked an eighth line on his sketchbook and knocked on his mother's bedroom door.

"Come in." Latisha was on her knees cleaning her carpet. The beige carpet was littered with burn marks.

"I have a question."

She turned to him. "About what?"

"How do I get a girl to talk to me?"

"Just go up to her and start a conversation."

"But what if she's mad at me?"

Latisha made a clicking sound with her tongue. "I got it! Draw her something. Girls love when guys draw cute pictures for them."

"Thanks." He jolted out the door and to the bus stop.

In first period, he watched the clock tick. Class was almost over, and Laila hadn't arrived. Raine knew it wasn't like her to be late. She was always the first person in class. He decided to wait until tomorrow to ask her what picture she would like drawn.

"Did you see my art in the newspaper?" asked Raine.

King was almost out of the classroom door. "Na. You won a contest or something?"

Raine walked next to him. "I drew at the live paint party Mrs. Kathy hosted."

"I'm not surprised; you're a beast when it comes to drawing."

"I wanted to show you the newspaper, but Laila got it."

King leaned back. "Laila?"

"Yeah. I'll catch you later," said Raine.

∞

Raine didn't understand how other classes dragged while time flew by in art class. He placed his painting on the counter and saw Laila's drawing. They were still working on portraits of family members. He saw a reference picture she used. He quickly snapped a picture of it.

"Mrs. Kathy, can I take home some supplies?"

"Of course. Take what you need. Raine?"

"Ma'am?"

"You have been working on this painting for a little over a week now. I've watched you complete work in a day. When are you going to fill in her face?"

He looked away. "I don't know."

"Do you need guidance?"

"Maybe."

"Elaborate, Mr. Landry."

Raine sighed. "I can't."

He didn't know how to explain to his teacher that he was conflicted on using the face of his drug addicted mom or the healthy mom from memory.

"I won't push but I expect you to finish up soon."

"Ok."

∞

Raine buttoned the last button on his shirt. He

used his hand to smooth it down then tucked it into his pants. His pants were ironed and creased. Most of his classmates complained about tucking in their shirts, but for Raine it was a sign of accomplishment. He had to leave his shirt untucked to sag his highwater pants. Now, his uniform fit perfect. He couldn't stop looking in the mirror at himself. He rushed to make sure he caught the bus.

"Ma, I'm headed out."

"Let me walk you to the bus stop."

Raine heard her fumbling around in her room. "No!"

She giggled. "Okay, how about I stand on the porch?"

Raine sighed. "Ok."

Latisha fixed his collar. "Is that for your girlfriend?"

"Yeah...she's not my girlfriend."

"Let me see." He handed it to her and she gasped. "This is beautiful. Looks like the picture."

They stepped onto the porch. "Who is it?" she asked.

"I don't know."

Latisha ran her hand over the woman's face. Her sleeve raised and sores on her arm were visible. She pulled her arm back and glanced behind him. "There's your bus."

She kissed his cheek and went into the house. Raine touched the spot she kissed. He marked a ninth line then ran to the bus stop.

He rushed into class with the picture. Laila was sitting in her desk sharpening her pencils. Raine shook his head. She was the only student excited about math class.

"Hey, Laila."

"Hi." She replied, without looking up.

"Man, this girl can hold a grudge", he thought.

He handed her the canvas. "I painted this for you."

She finally looked at him, tears pooled in her eyes. Raine pushed the painting into her shaky hands, wondering if she was upset that he drew the picture without her knowledge.

"Thank you," her voice broke.

"Why are you crying?"

She shrugged. "I love it."

Raine took his seat behind her. She stared at the picture until class started. That wasn't the reaction he hoped for, but at least she was talking to him again.

∞

Raine walked outside to the table expecting to see Laila, but the table was empty. He smacked his lips and sat down. *Probably with her little friends,* he thought. A few minutes later, Laila walked outside with Essence trailing her. Raine groaned. There was no way he was going to sit with Essence and listen to her squeaky voice. Raine watched Essence open her arms out wide and throw her head back. He decided to ignore their little fuss; besides he couldn't hear anyway. He failed at minding his own business, turning to watch them. Laila walked away from Essence, rounded the table, and sat opposite of him.

"What do you want?" he asked.

She raised a brow. "Eat your food, boy."

He looked away to hide his smile. The small things she did, like raise a brow, made his stomach flutter.

Laila pulled out a notebook and highlighted a few notes. She glanced over at him and smirked.

"Sleeping in class got you hungry?" she asked.

"Yep."

"Mr. Riker is giving us a test tomorrow."

"And?"

She rolled her eyes. "You should study." She read off her notes, trying to quiz him.

"Ay, girl. Don't spoil my appetite with schoolwork."

Laila laughed. Her face lighting up, revealing freckles under her eyes.

"You have freckles." Raine was intrigued. He had never seen a dark-skinned person with freckles.

"Yeah, so what?"

"Chill, I like it. I think I might add them to one of my new drawings."

That caused her to smile big. Raine looked away to keep himself from making googly eyes at her.

At the end of lunch, a few girls were passing out party flyers. Raine prepped himself for them to pass by him. He was surprised when they invited him.

"Are you going?" asked Laila.

"No."

"Why not?"

He shrugged. He wanted to believe the girls

invited him because he was okay to hang with, but he knew if he was still wearing the same uniform and shoes, they wouldn't bat an eye in his direction.

"Well, you wanna go so we can chill?"

Raine cleared his throat. "Um...yeah."

"Okay. I'll see you there."

∞

Raine picked up a cheap outfit from the store but the way his mother was carrying-on you'd think it was from some high-end fashion line.

"Look at my handsome, baby." She said for the millionth time.

She smiled at him through the cracked bathroom mirror. Each day she was looking better. Today was her tenth clean day. Raine hadn't seen her clean for this long in years. Even the men stopped coming.

"I'm gonna get you some sheets for your bed, and I'll get someone to replace that windowpane."

Raine refused to get his hopes up. Latisha sold everything in their home, but she made sure to keep her bed. For now, he was fine sleeping with the Barney blanket he'd had since he was a baby. As long as he wasn't on the hard and cold floor.

Raine pulled at his hair. "I should've gone to the barber shop."

"You look fine. What time are you coming home?"

"I don't know."

"Well, be safe," said Latisha. "Oh, I made an appointment for next Tuesday to get your shots."

"Thanks." Raine's eyes followed her out the bathroom door.

Although, he tried to remain positive, he was still waiting for the day she broke their promise. Remembering Mrs. Kathy's word, "Whether it's positive or negative, our thoughts become reality."

Think positive, he thought.

∞

The party wasn't hard to find. A few blocks away, he blended into the crowd being led there by the loud music. Raine walked to the entrance of the house party. He regretted not getting Laila's number. The entrance of the house and front yard were packed with people. Raine couldn't believe all the people there for freshmen.

"You want a drink?"

"No." Raine pushed the cup out of his face. He walked farther into the house and the smell of weed smothered his face. He quickly left the room but not before his head became fuzzy. He decided to go in the backyard for some fresh air.

The DJ was playing bounce music and had the crowd hype. The scene reminded Raine of the old painting of black people in a small club dancing. He wanted to remember the scene, so he could recreate it.

"For the culture," he announced.

"For the culture?"

Raine smiled when Laila walked up next to him. He held his hands up like a picture frame. "For the culture. This party scene."

Laila nodded. "I get it, Picasso."

"I'm surprised you know about Picasso with them stick figures you always drawing."

He laughed when she punched his side.

"Shut up!"

They watched the girls dance on tables. Raine laughed when one girl got on a table to dance but fell because the plastic table broke.

"You wanna go sit down?" Laila asked.

"Yeah."

They went into a side room away from the music. There were people sitting on the sofa, and the scene was a lot calmer than the backyard. Laila's eyes moved around the room. Raine took the opportunity to stare at her dark-brown skin and coiled hair.

"I'm surprised the police haven't shut this down. I can feel you staring at me." She glanced at him.

"Nobody staring at you."

"Um-hmm, let you tell it." She pointed to an empty table.

Raine followed eagerly behind her. Then sat opposite of her. They were quiet for a while until Laila cleared her throat.

"Wanna ask each other questions?" She asked Raine.

"Ok."

"Your favorite color?"

Raine tapped his chin. "Blue, green and gray. I can't choose between those."

"Why do you like those colors?"

"It's the colors I see on the levee and I go there

to clear my head. What's your favorite color?" he asked.

"Green."

"Why?"

"It was my mom's favorite color."

"Oh." Her response didn't make much sense to Raine, but he kept quiet.

Someone crashed into their table. "Oh, my fault."

Raine wiped liquor off his arm.

"Did I get you?" He leaned over and tried to help Raine.

"You good," Raine responded.

The boy looked over to Laila. "What's up, Laila?"

"Hey."

"I see you like wearing my chain."

Raine looked over at Laila and noticed she was wearing the same chain he seen dangling around the boy's long neck, the basketball chain.

She rolled her eyes. "You told me to bring it. I just wore it, so I wouldn't lose it."

"Whatever you have to tell yourself. Call me tonight."

"Nope," she responded, making her lip pop.

"We'll see about that."

Raine looked over at him. He had on expensive shoes, a name brand belt, a fresh haircut and didn't act nervous around her. Raine left from the table and went into the backyard. He tugged on the hem of his shirt and felt embarrassed that he even wore it. His clothes were plain compared to *him*.

"Why did you leave?" asked Laila.

He brushed her hand off his shoulder. "No reason."

Laila leaned her head. "What's wrong?"

"I'm leaving. I'll talk to you at school."

She pouted. "Already? It's because of Rashawn, huh?"

"No, I'm ready to go. Simple as that."

She crossed her arms. "Fine. Can you walk me home?"

Raine shrugged. "I don't care."

"Come on."

They walked down the steps and onto the sidewalk. The music grew softer.

"Raine?"

"What."

"Why are you mad at me?"

"I'm not mad." He picked up a rock and threw it. He didn't know how to get the anger out of his system, after watching her flirt with someone. Laila was still wearing the chain. He couldn't punch Rashawn because he didn't say anything to start a fight.

"Ow!" Someone yelled in the distance.

Laila grabbed Raine's arm and covered her mouth.

"Who threw this here rock?" asked the guy.

Laila grabbed his hand and they ran across the street and ducked behind a car. Raine kept putting a finger to his lips to quiet Laila down but that made her laugh louder. When they reached her house, she had tears falling from her eyes.

She held her stomach. "You almost got us beat up."

Raine laughed. "I swear I didn't see him."

She giggled a little more then got serious. "This is the first time I've heard you laugh."

Raine turned up his lip. "Go head."

"I'm serious." Laila walked up the steps and put her key in the door.

Raine turned to walk away, disappointed that their night had ended.

"Raine, come on."

"In your house?"

"No, I'm just holding the door open for the mosquitoes to come in. *Duh*."

Raine looked around and then back to the door, wondering if going into her house was the best move.

"Laila?" a voice called from inside the house.

"Yes, ma'am."

"Why are you standing in the door, child?"

Laila moved to the side. "Waiting on Raine to come in."

"Come on, sugar. You got her letting my cold air out."

Raine jogged up the porch and followed them into the house.

"What was your name again?"

Raine pulled his attention away from the pictures decorating her wall. "Raine."

"Raine, what?"

"Raine Landry."

"Landry...I know a few Landrys. What's your

mama's name?"

Raine glanced down at the floor. He debated on giving her a fake name. "Latisha Landry."

"Ok, yeah, I know Latisha. She used to walk around with a book in her hand as a child. I don't know how she saw where she was going."

Raine smiled. He was happy to hear a good memory of his mom and not the current rumors. He wondered if she knew his mom's current situation.

"I remember your grandma, Raeann Landry. Shame what happened to her."

Raeann? He finally had a name for his grandma. Now, he wondered what happened to her and why it made his mother cry.

"I'm Millie. You look different." She pointed to the wall. "And thank you for the picture. That's my daughter, Laila's mama."

She had hung the painting he did right in the middle of her wall, behind the sofa. He couldn't believe he missed it. He wanted to ask about his grandma but decided not to. He also wanted to know what she meant by looking different, but he didn't ask about that either.

"You're welcome," he said.

She went into the kitchen and retrieved another frame. "Here."

Raine grabbed the frame and saw that she had framed the newspaper article of him. She had even decorated the frame with his name.

"You look different in the newspaper picture," said Millie.

Raine tried to blink away a tear but it fell and landed on the frame. Millie rubbed his back.

"Thank you," he whispered.

He quickly wiped his face, mad that he was getting emotional in front of Laila and her grandmother. Millie pulled him into her arms and hugged him tight. Raine melted in her arms. When she tried to pull away, he leaned back in. Millie hugged him tighter and rubbed his back until he pulled away.

"I'm going to heat up some food. Y'all want some?"

"Yes, ma'am. I'm starving," said Laila.

"No, thank you," said Raine.

"I'll call when it's done," said Millie.

"Come on," said Laila.

She led the way to her room. "You can put your frame on the dresser."

Her room was mint green and white. Her bed was bigger than his mother's. He had to hop up to get on it.

Laila kicked off her shoes and joined him. "You can take off your shoes if you want."

"I'm good."

"Want to watch TV?"

"I don't really watch TV," said Raine.

"What? Why not."

"I haven't had one since I was about eight."

"A TV? Why not? Your parents that strict?"

"No."

"Then why?"

"Because my mama sold it when I was eight,

and I haven't had power in years. Well, until a few days ago."

He waited to see if she would laugh like everyone else.

"You can watch my TV and use my power whenever you want."

Raine squinted his eyes.

"Why are you looking at me like that?" asked Laila.

"I don't know."

They were quiet for a while.

"My grandma cried when I brought home your painting."

"Did your mama like it?"

She glanced at her hands. "My mama died a few weeks ago. That's why I had to move from Donaldsonville."

"I'm sorry. I didn't know." Now, he understood why she punched him when he called her drawing Mrs. Potato Head. *Smooth Raine*, he thought.

"I know."

"How did she die?" he asked.

"Car wreck. Why did your mom sell your TV?"

"It's getting late. I'm going to head out," said Raine, he rushed over to get the frame.

"Wait. I'll walk you out."

Raine walked out into the hallway without waiting for her. "Good night, Miss Millie."

"Leaving so soon?"

"Yes, ma'am." He was halfway out the door when he answered.

Raine continued down the steps and onto the

sidewalk. He heard Laila calling his name, but he continued on his way.

∞

Raine laid on the floor tossing his pencil in the air, trying to get ideas flowing for a sketch. Even though he loved his bed, he still felt more comfortable drawing on the floor. His ideas were blocked by Laila's question last night. He often wondered why his mother was a drug addict. She was normal until he turned eight. He often wondered if the stress of raising him caused her addiction.

"Hi."

Raine caught his pencil and sat up. "Hey."

Latisha walked over to him. "How was the party?"

"Cool."

She tapped his leg. "Get up."

"Na. I'm chillin' today."

Latisha dragged in a basket. "Picnic date?"

"Look, I don't wanna go." He grabbed his pencil and book and barged out the house onto the porch.

A picnic date? He scoffed at her mentioning those words. Picnics were a thing of the past. He paced on the porch trying to calm his nerves. After a few minutes, he was still angry. Raine decided to grab his book sack and go for a walk. He passed the kitchen and saw his mother sitting at the table with her head down. The basket and blanket rested next to her feet.

Raine sighed. "Ma, you still wanna go?"

"We can go another day." She smiled but he could see tears form in her eyes.

His stomach turned at her watery eyes. *Maybe I'm being too hard on her.* She did surprise him with new covers and pillows for his bed. She was trying for once. He decided to cut her a break.

He walked over to the table. "I hope you packed some sandwiches. I'm hungry."

She wiped her eyes and stood. "I packed your favorite. Let's go."

Raine locked the door and joined her on the sidewalk. He remembered trips to the levee being regular when he was younger. Latisha entangled their arms.

"I remember you were shorter than me. Now, I'm looking up to you."

"I know."

Latisha pointed out all the different kinds of trees and quizzed him on random stuff. She always made him think and as a child he hated it but now he longed for her pop quizzes.

"Crackhead Latisha." A young boy ran up to them and laughed.

Latisha put her head down. "Go find someone your age to play with, lil' boy."

Although she tried to be stern, Raine knew the kid had embarrassed her. He took a step toward the kid. His mother was more than a crackhead. She was more than an addiction and he was tired of hearing people make fun of her.

Latisha grabbed his arm and pulled him back.

"Boy, are you crazy? Are you going to hit that child?"

The boy ran towards his home.

"I wasn't gonna hit him. I was gonna scare him," said Raine.

"How?"

Raine walked past her. "Flip him upside down."

Latisha grabbed his arm and laughed. "You can't go around roughing up people's kids. You can't solve your problems with violence."

Raine jerked his arm away. "You can't solve your problems with drugs."

Latisha walked away. Raine debated on returning home. A picnic was a bad idea.

She spun around. "I know I have my shortcomings. I'm trying. Do I get credit for that?"

Raine sighed. He continued towards the levee. She was right.

On the levee, Latisha laid out their blanket and grabbed her book. Raine grabbed his sketchbook and listened to her read. He laid on his stomach while she was on her back. As she read the story, he sketched the characters from their descriptions.

"Ok. Let's see if we agree," said Latisha.

Raine handed his book to her. The character was described as having eyes like fire and hair that slithered around his head.

"Exactly how I imagined him," she said.

They stayed on the levee for hours reading and drawing like old times. His skills were so refined because she read to him and made him draw the characters. Raine marked an eleventh line in his book. He listened closely to her laugh, her conversation, and stored it in his mind.

CHAPTER 8

Raine got a text from Dizzy to meet at the shop. The last few jobs were at night or on the weekend, but Dizzy wanted them to meet at nine in the morning. Even though art was the only class he looked forward to, Raine was mad that he had to miss school. He was a "C" average student in all of his other classes. Raine decided that after today he was going to quit and find another way to pay Dolla.

Raine gave King a handshake. "Why do you have all that on?"

King was dressed in new shoes, a diamond chain, and had a custom platinum grill in his mouth.

King opened his arms and smiled showing off his grill. "Because I'm the man in these streets."

He dressed like the boy at the party. Raine thought they looked dumb, but girls didn't think so, even Laila. They headed to the shop and everyone they passed stared at King. A few girls stopped to talk to him, and one gave King her number.

"How long do you think we have to keep doing these jobs? I don't like missing school."

King shrugged. "I don't know. I'm not worried about school. I'm trying to get this money."

"I'm pulling out after this job."

"Dolla's not going to let you leave that easy."

"You owe him, not me. It's your fault I'm in this mess anyway."

"I didn't ask you to help me."

"No, but your mama did," Raine mumbled.

"What?" asked King.

"Man stop talking to me," said Raine.

"Whatever."

They walked the rest of the way in silence until King spoke.

"I saw your article in the paper. You sketch anything else?"

Raine reached for his sketchbook then decided against it. "No." He didn't want King to see the last two sketches were of Laila.

"Look, thanks for looking out for me," said King.

Raine nodded. He pulled the door open to the shop and saw the room was full of drugs, guns, and the same type of powder he often saw in his mother's room.

"Yo, Raine. Come here."

He walked up to Dizzy. "Yeah?"

"Take these bricks and load them in the duffle bags."

He hesitated, eyeing the drugs.

"Now," said Dizzy.

Raine did as he was told. As he worked on loading the bags, he wondered why he was doing all the work while King and TJ sat on the sofa looking at their phones.

"Strong from the weak," said Dizzy. He nodded in King and TJ's direction.

After loading all the bags, Raine and Dizzy climbed in the truck. Dizzy tossed TJ the keys to the shop and told him to watch the door. TJ mumbled something but didn't move. King was still on the sofa playing with his phone.

They got into the delivery truck and started down the road. Raine watched as they took the interstate towards Baton Rouge. He hoped they weren't going that far. Baton Rouge was two hours away. He stared out the window. After a while, the trees merged into blurry green specks like an oil painting.

"What ward you from?"

"Why?" Raine asked.

"You lucky I like you or I would've slap you in the head," said Dizzy.

"Whatever, man."

"Whatever, man," mocked Dizzy. "There he goes, twisting those dumb dreads."

Raine dropped his hand. "Why you sweatin' me?"

Dizzy laughed. "Because it's fun."

"How long you been working for Dolla?" asked Raine.

"Since I was ten," said Dizzy.

"How old are you now?"

"Sixteen."

"When do you go to school?"

"I haven't been to school since I was ten," said Dizzy. He turned up the radio. "Now, stop bothering me."

Raine rolled the window down and leaned on the door. The air was hot as it smacked against his face. He saw an exit sign for Donaldsonville and thought of Laila.

"That's where Donaldsonville is," he said.

"Yeah. You act like this is your first time out of New Orleans."

Raine continued to lean out the window. "It is."

"Roll the window up you're letting all that hot air in here," fussed Dizzy.

"Roll the window up," Raine mocked. "You sound like an old lady."

Dizzy let go of the wheel to put him in a headlock.

Raine yelled and grabbed the wheel. "Ay, man. Are you trying to kill us?"

Dizzy laughed. "No just you."

"Where are we going?"

"Baton Rouge," said Dizzy.

"Are we gonna be doing jobs in the morning too?"

"Why, crybaby? You have something else to do?"

"Yeah, school."

"Sometimes we do and sometimes we don't."

"I'm not doing anymore morning jobs," said Raine.

"You'll do whatever I say."

"I don't work for you, remember?"

"You work for me and I work for Dolla."

"No, we both work for Dolla, stupid."

Dizzy jumped at him. "Keep running your mouth."

"I'm not doing morning runs anymore."

"Well, tell that to Dolla. Since you work for him," said Dizzy.

"I will."

After the drive to Baton Rouge, Dizzy paid Raine a thousand dollars. He even paid TJ and King, but he let them know that it was because Dolla ordered him to and not by choice.

"You wanna go to the store? I need to buy some new shoes."

Raine looked at King's feet. "Those shoes are brand new."

"Are you coming or not?"

"Yeah."

Raine ran inside the shop to grab his book sack. When he turned around Dizzy gave him a bump.

"Little girl."

"What?" said Raine.

"I said you're a little girl."

Raine frowned. "I'm not a little girl. You wanna fight so I can prove it."

"You must be a little girl because you like playing dress up and pretend."

"Whatever, man." Raine left to catch up with TJ and King. On the way to the store, King and TJ talked about the shoes that had been released.

Raine didn't have a clue about the name or number of the shoes they talked about.

"Raine, what kind of shoes are you getting?" asked King.

"I don't know."

"Probably some Shaq's," said TJ.

"Raine, you remember you had some orange Shaq's?" said King. He was leaning on TJ laughing.

Raine ignored him. He remembered the shoes King was joking about. He had waited all night for his mother to return home. It was the night before school, and she promised to buy him some shoes. She returned around one that morning empty handed and high. Raine caught the bus to the 24-hour store and stole the first pair of shoes in his size. The store was quiet and empty, and he had to run for the bus when the manager saw him and gave chase. He was exhausted and kept nodding to sleep on the bus. When he got home it was after three in the morning, but he was glad that he had shoes to wear to school. TJ's laughter pulled him out of his daydream.

"I was clowning. He really had those ugly shoes?" TJ asked King like Raine wasn't walking next to them.

Raine walked up to TJ and took a swing. King stepped between them.

"Chill, Raine. We're just clowning."

TJ reached around King. "Let me get him."

"Y'all look real dumb right now. Chill!" King pushed TJ into the store. "Come on, Raine."

Raine went to the side opposite of TJ and

checked out the shoes. He decided on a pair of shoes that cost two hundred dollars. He didn't want to release the money to the cashier. King dragged him to a jewelry store to get a chain and a grill. Finally, they went to a barber shop. Raine decided on getting a fresh line and fade but kept the high-top dreads, twisting them had become his thing when he was nervous.

As Raine and King walked home, King let him know about his first football game. Raine was excited because he finally had money to get in and didn't need King to sneak him through the back gate.

∞

Raine slipped his sketchbook into his pocket as he sat in the backseat of Dizzy's car. The bass from Dizzy's speakers caused his lines to wiggle. Every kid they passed pointed at the car, and some even ran next to it.

"What time the football game starts?" asked Dizzy.

"Thirty minutes ago," said TJ.

Raine was on his way to the game when he saw Dizzy sped past. He spun the car around and told him to hop in.

"You mad? The game just started," said Dizzy.

"Bruh, I watch the game from the beginning to the end. You wanna stop and pick up Raine," said TJ.

"Stop crying." Dizzy reached up and turned the music back up.

Dizzy made another stop before driving to the game and TJ fussed the whole time. When they pulled up to the stadium, Raine heard the band mixed with cheering fans. The stadium was surrounded by darkness, but one foot through the gate, night turned into day. Under the stadium seats, were teenage members of The Family, posted on the concrete wall. Raine had to push through the crowd to follow Dizzy and TJ.

"I'm going to watch the game," said TJ.

Raine glanced around. Under the stadium was concrete walls blocking the view of the field. Raine thought it made no sense to go to a football game and not watch.

"Hey, Raine," a woman said.

Raine stepped forward and watched her walk past him. Her heels clicked on the concrete ground as she pulled at her mini skirt.

Raine's eyes widened. "Did she just say my name?"

The crew burst into laughter.

"Close your mouth, youngin'. She's too old for you," said the boy next to Dizzy.

Instead of heading up top with TJ, Raine headed in the direction of his admirer.

"I'm mature for my age," he said, making everyone laugh.

Dizzy put his hand on Raine's chest. "She knows your name because she *hangs* around the set. If you know what I mean."

Raine stared at the woman who was licking her lips and calling him over. He shook Dizzy off and headed her way. Dizzy sighed, and then punched Raine in the *boys*. Raine hurled over and grabbed his crotch.

"Argh." He tried to cuss but the words got stuck, sweat pooled on his forehead and vomit threatened to spill out. Raine released a high-pitched squeal.

Dizzy laughed. "Go watch the game with TJ."

Raine mugged Dizzy. He gave the woman another glance before limping off.

"Tell your girl, bye," said Dizzy.

Raine headed up the bleachers and scanned for TJ. He spotted him and jogged up the cement steps.

TJ snatched him down. "Move; I can't see."

Raine groaned and wiped sweat from his forehead.

TJ looked at him for a second before his eyes dashed back to the field. "What's wrong with you?"

"Dizzy punched me in the nuts."

TJ laughed. His attention still on the game. "For real? Why?"

"Some woman tried to holla at me. She knew my name and everything."

"She had on a mini skirt and heels?"

"How you know?"

He patted Raine's shoulder. "Everybody knows her."

"What's King doing?" asked Raine.

"He ran for fifteen yards, but they haven't given him the ball since."

"GO!" someone yelled.

Raine watched King take off down the field, spinning and breaking tackles.

"Number six, King Brooks, is in for the touchdown," said the announcer.

Raine and TJ stood and clapped with the crowd.

"My boy a beast," said Raine.

"Yep, they need to give him the ball more."

"Trevin, is that you?" A white man sat down next to TJ. He took the cap off revealing a tan line on his forehead.

TJ shifted. "Hey, Coach."

"Where have you been, son?"

"Chillin'."

"You were my starting quarter back and you just disappeared on us."

TJ sighed. "I told you I had to move because of family issues."

"You did, but I have been checking rosters for your name and I haven't seen you on any. Why are you not playing?"

TJ stood. "I'll see you around, Coach." He jogged down the steps and disappeared under the stadium.

"King Brooks is in for another touchdown!" yelled the announcer.

"Do you have any contact info on Trevin?" asked the Coach.

Raine reached in his pocket for the phone. There was no harm in giving him TJ's number. Raine shook his head and removed his hand.

"Na."

"Well, tell him I still have a spot for him."

"I will," said Raine. "I have to go."

He jogged down the steps in the same direction TJ went to tell him what the coach said.

∞

Raine missed school on Monday dealing with Dizzy. He was relieved that they didn't have to do anything this morning because he wanted to see Laila and go to art class.

"Where's your chain and new shoes?" asked King.

They were standing on the corner waiting on the school bus. King had his hair braided in a zig zag pattern and had jewelry draped over his body.

"In my book sack."

King frowned. "In your book sack?"

Raine whispered. "Yeah, so my mama wouldn't steal it."

"Why didn't you put it on?"

"I don't know."

King shrugged. "More girls for me."

Raine laughed. "Shut up."

Raine and King looked down at their vibrating phones.

Dizzy: Meet at shop ASAP

Raine heard the bus roaring towards them. The thick morning fog blocked his view, but the bus lights flashed through the gray fog. The bus rolled to a stop in front of them and extended the yellow arm.

"Raine, are you coming?" asked King.

"Are you getting on, son?" asked the bus driver.

Raine looked at the bus driver, planted in his seat, and then at King. The steps on the bus seemed to be getting farther away. He walked out of the bus line and over to King. Instead of getting on, they crossed the street in front of the bus and headed to the shop.

"I wonder what Dizzy want," said King.

"Same thing he always wants. For me to help destroy lives. That's what he wants!"

"Calm down, boy."

"I am calm...boy." He walked up to King with his fist clenched, ready to punch him.

King smacked his lips and walked off. "You trippin'."

∞

Raine was in the backseat of a car with King, while Dizzy and TJ sat up front. Dizzy had him switch the license plate and scratch off a number on a sticker. He was sure the car was stolen. Dizzy didn't give them any clue about where they were going. They had passed the Louisiana state line hours ago.

He didn't get a chance to tell TJ what the coach said. When he found TJ, he was under the bleachers surrounded by members. Raine decided to tell him when they got to their destination.

"Let me get some of that," said King.

TJ was smoking weed in the passenger seat while Dizzy drove and rapped to Soulja Slim. TJ extended the weed to King. He pulled on it and started choking. His braids swung back and forth as his head jerked. Raine patted him on the back and let the window down.

"Stupid," said Raine. King would be kicked off the football team if he tested positive for marijuana.

"Give back my blunt, youngster," said TJ.

Raine saw a sign that had Mississippi on it.

"Where are we going?" asked Raine. Dizzy turned up the radio and ignored him. Raine watched out the window until he drifted off to sleep.

WACK.

Raine jumped up and looked around. Dizzy had the car door open and was standing over him.

"Smack me again," yelled Raine.

Dizzy laughed and walked off. "Come on, cry baby."

They had pulled up to a hotel. Raine followed Dizzy, but he made sure to take in the hotel; it was the tallest building he had ever seen.

"You act like you're in New York or something. Tripping all over your feet looking at the building. It's only seven floors," said Dizzy.

Raine followed him through the revolving doors, hesitating too long and causing the door to stop. Dizzy looked back at him and laughed.

"I broke it?" he asked Dizzy.

"Bruh, you are slow. It stopped to keep from smashing your ignorant ass. Watch…"

The door started to spin again. Raine made sure not to get too close to the glass. He jumped out the door and into the lobby, stumbling into Dizzy. King and TJ were in the lobby laughing at him.

Raine huffed and headed in their direction. "What's so funny?"

"We did the same thing. King kept making the emergency switch stop the door. He was walking too slow then too fast," said TJ.

Raine relaxed and sat next to them while Dizzy checked in with the woman at the desk. Raine heard her ask about school. Dizzy flirted with her and flashed a few bills. He got her number and the room card. They headed to their room. Dizzy barely had the door open when King ran in and jumped on the bed. He was touching everything in the room. The phone, TV remote, he even wrote on the little notepad.

King grabbed the Bible out of the nightstand and placed his hand on Raine's head. "Bow your heads," he said, making Raine and TJ laugh.

Dizzy rubbed his head. "I should've got King his own room. Sit down!"

"Ay, room service free, right?" asked King, with the phone in his hand.

"No. You order, then you pay for it," said Dizzy.

"Man, movies be lying," said King. He laid across the bed and pouted.

"You mean to tell me, movies aren't real?" asked TJ and laughed.

"What we did in New Orleans was childish stuff and y'all didn't have my back. I need y'all to look confident this time. We don't have to do anything but watch Dolla in action," said Dizzy.

"Any questions?" asked Dizzy; they all looked at

Raine.

"As long as no one gets hurt," said Raine.

"You worried about the wrong thing. An enemy of Dolla's is an enemy of you. That enemy gets hurt, then better him than you," said Dizzy.

"Whatever," said Raine.

"Whatever? You either have our backs or you don't. You're either all in or not. I don't see you complain when you get paid for jobs," said Dizzy.

Raine looked away. He was right. After joining, he had new clothes and a new bed. He was better off since joining The Family.

"Anyway, we don't have to go with Dolla until tonight. Dolla put us here because there's a beach out back. We can hit the gift shop and get some clothes." He pulled out rolls of money and tossed it to each of them. "This trip is on Dolla."

∞

Raine, King, Dizzy and TJ stood at the edge of the beach. They had swim trunks on and towels wrapped around their necks. Raine had dreamed of sitting on a beach sketching in the sand with the sun warming his face.

"This ain't what a beach supposed to look like," said TJ, frowning.

"For real, I be seeing them on TV. This water ain't blue and the sand ain't tan," said King.

"What the hell is that? It's covered in mustard greens!" yelled Dizzy.

"That's not mustard greens, dumbass, it's seaweed," said Raine.

Dizzy grabbed Raine and put him in a headlock while King and TJ laughed.

"Let me go. I don't wanna fall in this," said Raine.

"For real, Dizzy, stop kicking this sand up, it might cause cancer," said TJ.

King grabbed a handful of sand and threw it on them. He took off running to the hotel with them chasing after him. Dizzy was cussing and threatening King. Raine was last because he couldn't stop laughing at Dizzy.

"Last one getting locked out the room," said TJ.

They all slid through the door and ran to the stairs instead of the elevator. Raine got to the floor and heard the room door slam. He banged on the door.

"Stop playing!"

"What's the password," said King.

"Open the door before I smack all y'all," said Raine.

He heard them laugh, but they didn't open the door.

"Stop playing before we get kicked out," said Raine.

King opened the door for him. Raine pushed him and sat down on the bed.

"I'm about to take a nap," said Dizzy.

"Old lady," Raine mumbled, but Dizzy heard him and slapped his head.

"Raine, look at this." King held up a museum brochure. "It's right down the street. Wanna go?"

They all looked at Dizzy. "Na."

Raine sighed.

"Let them go. We need to see if ol' girl got a friend," said TJ, referring to the desk clerk.

"Go, but don't get into anything. KING."

"Chill," said King.

Raine and King walked around the museum for two hours looking at pottery and paintings. In one gallery, King said, "You're gonna be famous one day with art in a museum."

King may not have known the impact his words had on Raine. He felt proud that his best friend thought he could make it. When they got back to the hotel, TJ told them to chill with him in the lobby. Raine thought it was the perfect time to tell TJ what his old coach said.

"King, see if they have some place to eat here."

"You go," said King.

Raine whispered. "I need to holla at TJ." King nodded and walked outside.

"Remember that white dude, the coach, he said he still has a spot for you," said Raine.

TJ looked up from his cell phone with a scowl. He jumped up and Raine did the same. TJ bumped into him knocking him back onto the sofa. Anger rushed through Raine. He stumbled back to his feet.

"What's your problem?" asked Raine. He followed TJ and yanked his jersey. "I said, what's your problem. You're always wearing these football jerseys. There's a coach that wants you on his team."

TJ walked out the door, punching the palm of his hand. "I can't do that. My father wants me training to take over the business."

"Tell him you don't wanna do it."

TJ took a deep breath. "Imagine Dolla times five."

Raine nodded. "There has to be a way."

"I have to leave practice or miss games for this stuff. No coach will put up with that."

"King does it."

"How long do you think that will last?" asked TJ. "I wish I could trade places with you."

"Now I know you're trippin'."

"You're free to do and go wherever you want. Your family don't have expectations for you, and no family name to live up to."

Raine stared at the ground. He knew TJ was trying to make a point but downing him wasn't the way.

"I'm free to do as I please because my mama was too high to care. That's not a life to envy."

He handed TJ the sketch he'd made. TJ was wearing a jersey but this time it had his name on it.

"Stand up to your dad or continue doing this for the rest of your life, but don't you ever mention my family."

∞

Dolla was in line with the other bosses in front of Dizzy, TJ, King and Raine. Each boss had their trusted crews standing behind them. Raine felt tiny compared to the other group to his left and right. They were filled with grown men with muscular bodies and tattooed arms. They were the only kids in the room.

Apparently, Dolla worked for someone also and he wasn't happy. Raine thought the head boss looked like a warrior. His long dreads hung down to his butt.

"Dolla, you and your Rugrats good?" asked the head boss. The other crews laughed.

Dolla glanced back. "My Rugrats got more heart than any of these grown men. Especially, Dizzy. You know I been grooming him since he was ten, Pep. Youngin' with the dreads is next."

Raine's heart sped. Dolla was grooming him to be in the gang for life not to pay him back and leave.

"Whatever you say. Now, I just denied some cats a whole lot of money. I got a feeling the streets are about to get hot. I brought y'all here because the people I denied have crews set up in each of your cities. As you know, my brother and sister-in-law was killed last month. The police called it an accident, but we know better. That situation was handled. Now, we have more people at our necks. I'm giving y'all extra heat for the coming problems. I don't want to lose any of you because you're my blood. So, be safe and let me know if you need more *tools*," said Pep.

After the meeting, Raine sat off to the side watching Pep's people load Dolla's vans with brown boxes. Raine sighed, thinking New Orleans didn't need any more guns on the street. He watched Dolla and TJ laugh and clown with their uncle, Pep, and their cousins.

How can they laugh at a time like this? he thought. Pep had just told them that they needed to be prepared for war. Raine had refused to kill anyone and he hadn't changed his mind. No beating Dizzy or TJ gave him could change that. *I have to figure a way out of this*, he thought.

Feeling the urge to vomit, he leaned forward and threw up. The sound caused everyone to look his way. Raine spat and took a seat on the side.

TJ walked over to him and sat next to him. "You straight?"

Raine nodded. "Yeah, probably something I ate."

"I'm gettin' that drawing tatted on my arm."

Raine nodded.

"Look, I meant no disrespect to your family. What I meant was you have a clean slate. You can be anything you wanna be."

"Junior, come here!"

TJ walked over to a guy with the same midnight skin tone as Dolla. Except, he towered over everyone standing next to him. The man said something that made everyone laugh except TJ.

King walked over to him and laughed. "TJ's dad is tall."

Raine understood why TJ didn't stand up to him. He was like Jackson on steroids. Raine pulled out his sketchbook and drew TJ and his father. In the picture, TJ towered over his father.

∞

The next day at school, Raine rushed outside to the table and saw Laila eating with her head down. She had her notebook open next to her plate. After leaving Louisiana for the first time, he had to tell someone, and Laila was the first person he thought about.

"What's up?" He sat across from her.

Laila continued eating.

He waved his hand in front of her face. "Hello?"

Laila flipped over a page in her notebook. Raine waited for a few seconds. He continued to stare at her.

"Be that way." He stood from the table and headed for the door. He slowed his pace then headed back to her. Being nice didn't work, but he knew how to make her talk.

He walked over to her and picked up her spoon. He shoveled her gumbo into his mouth, making sure to slurp. He smirked when Laila turned up her nose and slammed her book closed. He folded his arms and prepared for her mouth.

He watched her chest rise and fall. She opened the book and resumed eating. Raine's mouth dropped. His smile faded. *How could she not go off?* He twisted a dread with a brow raised. Finally, he reclaimed his seat across from her.

Laila closed her book and looked up at him. "You can't bully me."

Raine nodded. "I wanted to tell you that I saw a Donaldsonville sign on the way to Baton Rouge."

"Why did you run away from my house?" she asked.

"Why did you eat that gumbo after I ate from your spoon?"

"Are you poison?" she asked.

"No."

Laila shrugged. "Then what's the big deal?"

Raine shook his head. No one ate after him, not even King.

"One time I ate at King's house, his mama gave me plastic stuff, but she gave the other dudes *real* plates and spoons."

"Maybe, she ran out of plastic to give them."

Raine laughed. "I got my food first and she didn't want to give me that. King made her. People don't trust me enough to eat after me."

Laila frowned. "I'm not *people*. I don't care about that."

"No? Then why do you wear different shoes every other day and why do you hang with greasy lips?"

Laila smiled. "My brother buys me shoes every time something new drops and *Essence* was the only person that talked to me on my first day."

Raine pulled out the cheap sketchbook since Jackson ripped his special one. He handed her the book.

"I drew the sign and added some girly flowers around it."

Laila turned away and wiped her eyes. Raine snatched the book from her and ripped the page out.

"Here, you can have it, just don't cry."

Laila giggled and held her arms out.

Raine leaned back. "What?"

"I want a hug, Raine."

"Why?"

Laila rolled her eyes. "Forget it."

She shoved her notebook into her book sack, then gently placed the drawing inside. Raine put his sketchbook into his pocket and stood. He scratched his neck as he watched her walk away, getting farther out of reach.

Maybe letting her stay mad was for the best. Now, she couldn't ask questions about his mama. He headed in the opposite direction but found himself running to catch her.

"Wait up." He jogged up next to her and pulled her into a hug. She smelled like cotton candy. Raine closed his eyes and smiled. When he opened his eyes, his face twisted up. He pretended to vomit. Essence smacked on a piece of gum, the sun making her greasy lips shine more. She tapped Laila on her shoulder.

"Um, Laila, everyone's looking for you."

Laila pulled away. Her eyes danced from Raine to Essence. "I'll see you in art class."

She backed away but Raine didn't want to release her hand.

Essence stomped her feet. "Girl, come on."

Raine smirked when she walked away. He couldn't wait to get out of school to go to the levee and draw Laila.

∞

Raine stared out the window while the bus dropped everyone off. The green leather seats were sticky and smelled like old books. All the windows were down on the bus but sweat poured down his face. He had his sketchbook on his lap planning to head straight to the levee.

"Mr. Clarence, you need to push this bus. My whole shirt wet," said King.

"Get somewhere and sit down. We all know it's hot, but you need to state the obvious."

"Whatever," said King.

"Cut that hair off your head. I bet you wouldn't be hot," said Mr. Clarence.

Raine shook his head. King would never cut his hair. He grew braids because his father had them.

Raine jumped when someone plopped down in the seat with him. Laila wiped sweat from her forehead and smiled.

"What are you doing on my bus?"

"Your bus, your table. You do know none of that is for you."

Raine laughed. "What are you doing here?"

She used her thumb to point behind her. "Essence and Lewis getting off at King's house."

"You too?"

"I was until I saw you."

Raine's palms matched his forehead. The bus stopped and Raine stood. "This is my stop."

Laila grabbed her book sack and walked ahead of him. They all got off the bus and walked along the sidewalk. Raine headed across the street to his house and Laila followed.

"Where are you going? King lives down there," said Essence, while eyeing Raine.

"Just text me when you're ready," said Laila. "I'm chillin' with Raine."

Lewis turned up his nose. "Why?"

Raine took a step towards Lewis, "Don't worry..."

"Why are you worried about them? She wanna chill with him then let her," said King.

Raine backed away and gave King a quick head nod.

"Can I use your bathroom?" Laila asked.

"You just left from school. There's like twenty toilets there."

"First of all, I didn't have to use it then."

Raine glanced over at his house. The grass was as high as the porch. The screen door was hanging sideways, and the paint peeled from the trimming. *Why would she want to go inside?* he thought. His house was great for October but for the other months it stuck out.

"I'm locked out until my mama get home."

"Oh."

"I'll bring you over to King's house."

Raine sat on the porch outside of King's house waiting for Laila. He stood then sat down again.

"I should leave before she comes back," he mumbled.

Raine tried to come up with an excuse for Laila. She wanted to *chill*, but he was worried about bringing her inside his home. Raine jumped up when King's door opened.

"You're a pretty lil' black thang," said Kia. Her smile dropped when she saw Raine. "King is busy with his friends."

"Good, because I'm not here for him. Ready?"

Kia watched with wide eyes as Laila walked down the steps towards Raine.

"Nice meeting you," said Laila.

Kia leaned her head. "You're not staying?"

"No, ma'am."

Raine smirked. He grabbed Laila's hand and walked across the street.

"So, what are we doing?"

Raine dropped her hand. "Um…I was headed to the levee."

"The levee? For what?"

"Watching the water helps me relax."

Laila frowned. "That brown water?"

Raine laughed. "I imagine it's blue with sand surrounding it."

"I image it's brown with alligators."

"Girl, you comin' or not?"

Laila grabbed his hand. "Lead the way." A few seconds later, Laila glanced at him. "King's mom didn't call you his friend. Why?"

Raine shrugged. "She doesn't like me."

"Duh, but why."

"She thinks I'm the reason King gets into trouble."

"Everyone knows King is a troublemaker."

"Except her," said Raine.

"Well, you should tell her it's King."

"King can do no wrong in her eyes, so it wouldn't make a difference."

"You don't know that," said Laila.

"Look, I don't wanna talk about that anymore." She rubbed her arm. "Ok."

"Miss Mille let you come over here?"

Laila smirked. "I told her I was studying with Essence."

"She knows it's a lie."

Laila's smile dropped. "No, she doesn't, or I wouldn't be here."

"You like to study alone, even I know that."

Laila glanced away. "She doesn't know. I hope she doesn't know."

Raine laughed as they walked up the steps and sat on a bench. Laila closed her eyes. "Bahamas, Bahamas..." She opened her eyes and frowned. "BB"

"BB? What's that?"

"Barges and brown water."

Raine laughed. "So, you don't see Hawaii in front of you?"

Laila touched his forehead. "Do you need a doctor?"

Raine knocked her hand down and pulled out his sketchbook. "I'm going to draw it."

Thirty minutes later, Raine put his pencil colors back into the case. The heat from the sun had put Laila to sleep fifteen minutes ago. She was leaned into his side curled under him. He wiped sweat from her forehead and ran his hand across her face.

"Wake up."

She sat up and stretched. "You done?"

"Stare at the water," he said. While she looked, he slid the drawing in front of her face.

She gasped. "How did you do that? You turned the barges into sandcastles and the trees into islands. Look at the water. You're so talented."

"Thanks."

Raine and Laila sat on the levee until Essence called her. Her voice through the phone prompted an eye roll from him. He wasn't mad for long because he knew he would see her at school.

∞

Raine missed school days last week dealing with The Family. Now, he was in the waiting room of a clinic. Latisha had walked out forty-five minutes ago. Raine checked outside for her a couple times before sitting back down in the chair.

He heard a young boy whine. He looked up to see his mother hug him tight and rub his back, calming the child. He looked away when the mother looked his way. The baby reminded him of Joshua.

A nurse yelled over screaming babies. "Raine Landry."

Raine glanced at the door one more time before following behind the nurse. She took his height and weight and brought him to a room.

"What brings you by?"

"I need to get some shots."

"We will need a parent or guardian present before we can administer them. You are pretty far behind on your shots. Is your parent in the waiting room?"

Raine bit his lip. "No."

"Who will sign…?"

"My mom is in the next room with my little sisters."

"Well, come on. I can put y'all in the same room."

Raine exhaled. "I need some space. I'm always surrounded by girls. I have four sisters."

The nurse smiled. "Believe me, I understand. I have three big brothers."

She placed a paper on the table. "Just have your mother sign the paper before the doctor comes in and we'll get you all caught up."

"Thank you."

After she exited the room, Raine went over to the paper and signed Latisha's name. He got three shots and a prescription for vitamins because he was underweight. Raine took the prescription and the shot record and rushed to the door before the staff figured out his mother wasn't there.

He walked around the block a few times, worried something had happened to her. He walked around until it was time to catch the bus.

∞

Raine jogged up the steps and walked into the house. The door was slightly open.

"Let's go before they leave."

Raine's stomach turned when he heard Jackson's voice.

"Give me a second."

"Hurry up, girl. You got $200 and act like you afraid to use it."

Raine was in the middle of the door, watching as Jackson entered the hallway. Jackson smirked when he noticed Raine. His mother was behind Jackson counting money.

"Now, who's moving slow," said Latisha.

Jackson stepped to the side to let Latisha pass. She froze when she saw Raine at the door.

"Hey…Rainbow. When did you get here?" she stuttered.

"Where did you go?" asked Raine.

"I wasn't feeling well, so I came home."

"You left a clinic where there's doctors?" asked Raine.

Latisha scratched her head. "You know I don't be thinking."

"Where did you go, Ma?"

Jackson grabbed Latisha. "We don't have time for this mess."

Raine pulled out his sketchbook and shoved it in her face. "Today is line thirteen. Thirteen days clean."

Latisha walked past him. "I'll be right back."

Raine let out a hoarse *Ma*. His body felt weak, so weak his voice got caught in his throat. He ripped out the page from his book and threw it on the floor. He walked into his room but paused. His mother had stolen his bed and dresser and sold it.

She did it again. Every time he saw a little light, she would snatch him right back down into darkness. Raine slammed the room door shut and left.

CHAPTER 9

Raine spat in the sink then wiped his mouth. He slammed his toothbrush on the counter.

"Morning, Rainbow."

"Don't call me that."

He pushed past her and headed for the door.

"I'm sorry about yesterday. I got off track, but I'm getting myself together."

Raine scoffed and kept moving. He jogged down the steps and met up with King.

King tugged at his chain. "That's what I like to see."

Raine had a chain on and a platinum grill in his mouth along with the new shoes he bought. Yesterday, he went to the barbershop and got designs in his fade like the cool kids. At the bus stop a few football players complimented Raine's shoes. They even held a conversation with him instead of acting like he didn't exist.

At school, Raine was in the hall with King and his crew. King always stood along the lockers to mess with girls. Raine didn't see the point, but now he understood why King did it. A few girls spoke to him, but he was waiting for Laila. He leaned off the locker and grabbed her hand as she passed. She frowned until she realized it was him. Her eyes scanned over his hair, chain, and shoes. She rolled her eyes and yanked her arm away.

Raine gave King the finger when he laughed. He chased after her, yelling her name.

"What's up with you?"

She pushed him. "Get away from me."

"Why?"

She glanced at his mouth. "You look stupid. You can't even talk with that grill in your mouth. You look more like King than Raine."

"Well, a few girls like it."

"Go talk to them." Laila pulled the classroom door open and went in.

Raine snatched the grill out of his mouth and followed her. He remembered how much she smiled at Rashawn and he was dressed the same way. She even wore his chain.

He sat behind her. "All right, be that way."

He placed the grill back in his mouth and pulled out his phone. He kept his attention on the phone throughout the math lesson. Most days he tried to pay attention and learn enough to pass the test, but he wasn't in the mood to hear about how to find "X".

∞

In art class, Raine was putting the finishing touches on his portrait, with each stroke he was becoming tenser. Laila kept glancing at him but didn't say anything and that made him angrier. Raine wished someone called him dirty or did anything to him today, but no one stepped out of line. Even the compliments on his shoes were making him mad.

"Are you okay?" Laila asked.

She continued. "Can I borrow your pencil?"

Raine continued to paint like she wasn't talking. She wanted to talk now, but he was still embarrassed about earlier.

Mrs. Kathy walked behind him. "I see you finally finished the face."

She leaned her head to the side. "Looks a bit rough but I love it. What's her name?"

Raine dropped the brush. He mumbled something too low to hear.

"What was that?" asked Mrs. Kathy.

"I said her name is Crackhead!" Raine grabbed his stuff and stormed out the class.

∞

Raine pulled his vibrating phone from his pocket and saw a text from Dizzy.

Dizzy: Meet at the shop ASAP

Raine pushed through the school's doors and headed to the bus stop. Any other day he would've been mad, but Dizzy's text was welcomed. He was looking forward to hitting the road with Dizzy. He needed to get away from New Orleans.

When he walked in, Dizzy pulled him to the side. Dolla was at the pool table whispering with

Raine

Tape and a few other guys. Raine could feel the tension as soon as he walked in.

"Dizzy, you and your crew come here," said Dolla.

Dizzy motioned for Raine to follow him.

"Where the other two?"

"On the way," said Dizzy.

"Tape's brudda was hit by some people from ninth ward. I need y'all to hit back."

"He alive?" asked Dizzy.

"Na, man. He died a few hours ago," said Dolla. "Soon as dark falls. Light it up."

Raine sat on the couch and started sketching to calm his mind, but it wasn't working. Like painting the picture in art class didn't help earlier. Dizzy sat next to him and watched him draw for a few seconds.

"That's tight."

"Thanks," said Raine.

"I saw your lil' ugly self in the newspaper too."

"I didn't know you read."

Dizzy put him in a headlock.

"I meant to say, I didn't know you read newspapers," said Raine. "Let me go."

Dizzy laughed but released him. "I read the paper every morning."

"Oh."

"Look, if you still want out, now is the time. Before we do this. Talk to Dolla and see what he says."

Raine released a deep breath. Dizzy was right, he had to get out now. When Raine stood, his sketchbook dropped to the floor. The book fell open to the page he ripped out after his mother left to get high. The same day she sold his bed, now he was sleeping on the floor again. It was only a matter of time before she started selling their food.

Raine snatched the book off the floor. He always struggled, went to sleep with a headache from not eating, lived without power and running water. He was always called the *dirty one* because of his mother.

Raine sat down. "Forget it."

∞

Raine's heart raced at the sound of guns being loaded.

Dizzy elbowed him. "Here."

Raine's shaky hands reached for the gun. He thought of a million ways to get out of the moving car, but his body was frozen. Dizzy motioned for him to calm down. He extended the gun again. Raine snatched the gun. The weight of the gun surprised him. He could barely hold it with both hands.

Dizzy grabbed his arm. "The safety isn't on, so watch where you point it."

Raine pointed the gun towards the floor. His job was to help Dizzy and King shoot while TJ drove. Dizzy was in the passenger seat while he and King were in the back.

King loaded the gun like it was nothing. He

pulled the mask down over his face and leaned over the seat. Raine only saw flashes of their motions because it was so dark. The occasional streetlight lit the car enough for him to see that TJ's arm was shaking, Dizzy's mask was a little crooked, and King's eyes dashed around.

"Here we go. Get ready," said TJ.

Raine noticed they were in the same spot he had painted the wall. In front of the wall he saw a shadow, crouching low, moving slow. He leaned in to get a closer look.

"Wait…" said Raine.

The shadow raised his arm and blew fire from his palms. Raine slid down into the seat and covered his ears. His mask was still rolled up on his head.

"They were waiting on us," yelled TJ. "I'm getting out of here."

He slammed on the breaks and put the car in reverse.

"No! Keep driving," said Dizzy.

"You don't hear them shooting at us," yelled TJ.

Glass shattered sprinkling over Raine's head.

"We can't go back; they blocked us in," said Dizzy. "Now, keep driving before they pin us in from the front too."

Raine drop the gun and closed his eyes as Dizzy and King fired out the window. His eyes popped open at the sound of chaos. He watched as shells flew from King's gun. TJ yelled, and the car swerved to the right running over a curb. Raine was penned to the floor when King was thrown on him.

King sat up and pulled him from the floor.

Dizzy grabbed the wheel. "Pull TJ in the back."

Raine and King struggled to get TJ over the seat. TJ had blood spilling from his body. Raine couldn't tell where he was shot.

TJ mumbled as tears fell down his face. His eyes were wide as he grabbed and twisted Raine's shirt.

"Get us out of here," yelled King. He snatched the mask off and wiped his eyes.

"Dolla, it was a set-up. They were waiting for us. TJ got hit," Dizzy yelled into the phone, while driving like a mad man.

"Hold on," said King to TJ.

Raine stared down at TJ. He was quiet now, gasping for air. Raine had one hand on the door handle and one hand clasping TJ's hand. TJ was no longer grabbing his shirt or squeezing his hand. They pulled up to a parking lot where Dolla was already waiting and got out of the car. Dolla had some guys carry TJ to another car.

"Let's go. Run through every traffic light," said Dolla as he jumped in the car.

The tires screeched when they pulled off. Raine watched the taillights until he couldn't see them anymore. His legs felt weak when he saw that he was covered in TJ's blood.

"Raine, give me the gun," said Dizzy.

Raine was in a trance as he looked down at the gun. A tear dropped onto the black handle. He hadn't realized he was holding it until then. He turned to Dizzy and pointed the gun at him. Raine quickly wiped his face with the other hand. His body trembled, and his hand shook so much the gun rattled.

King took a step back. "Raine, what are you doing?"

Dizzy threw his hands up in surrender. "Hand me the gun."

Raine tightened his hand around the handle. Slowly, Dizzy walked closer to Raine and allowed the gun the touch his chest. He snatched the gun from Raine's hand.

The streetlights blurred and now they looked like stars; Raine felt like he could almost touch one. He reached out and closed his eyes…

∞

Raine jumped to his feet.

"You are one simple lil' boy. You know that, right?" Dizzy whispered. He walked closer and snatched him back down on the sofa.

"What happened?" Raine whispered. He was back at the shop.

"You fainted with your arm stretched out looking stupid. I should've left you like that."

"What time is it?" asked Raine.

"Two in the morning."

He glanced up and saw Dolla and a few people huddled around the pool table. King was sleeping on the couch also. Dolla called Dizzy over. Raine nudged King and King jumped awake. His eyes were red with white streaks down his face. He scooted closer to Raine. They both looked up as Dizzy cussed out loud and kicked the pool table.

He rushed past Dolla.

"I'm dropping y'all off, so get your stuff," said Dizzy.

Raine grabbed his book sack and followed Dizzy and King to the car. Raine stared out the window during the quiet drive to their house. The drive-by didn't seem real. TJ getting shot had to be a part of a nightmare.

"TJ didn't make it," said Dizzy.

Raine wiped his nose then eyes as he stared ahead. TJ was gone, and it was their fault. He and TJ weren't best friends, but he didn't deserve to die behind beef his uncle created.

"Right here," said Raine.

Dizzy pulled up to his house. The car was still rolling when King jumped out and walked over to his house.

"I froze during the shoot out."

Dizzy shrugged. "I didn't need you getting in the way anyway."

Raine looked out the window and noticed Jackson on the steps. Raine tightened and released his fists a couple times while staring at Jackson. He pulled the door open and got out. "Thanks."

Raine tried to walk past him but Jackson wouldn't move.

"Did you see your no-good mama?"

"Move out my way."

Jackson jumped up and grabbed Raine by his hair. He laughed at Raine swinging wild and missing. At that moment, Raine wished he still had the gun. He heard a car door slam and then a gun cock.

"Let him go."

Raine moved away from Jackson and got behind Dizzy.

Jackson put his hands up and backed away. "Tell your mama I'll be back for my cut."

"That's your pops?" asked Dizzy. He tucked the gun away.

"Hell no."

"Go in the house. I'm out," said Dizzy.

Raine did as told and walked into the dark house. He flicked the switch and realized the power was off again. He walked into his room and grabbed his old blanket and laid on the floor. No lights, no bed, and no mother.

∞

The school day seemed to drag on, even in art class. Raine ignored Laila and Mrs. Kathy whenever they tried to hold a conversation. He didn't know why he was mad at Mrs. Kathy and he felt bad for being rude to her. After art class, he got a text from Dizzy, so he headed to the shop. King walked along with him.

"Lewis said somebody in ninth ward got shot in the shoot-out."

Raine's heart raced. "Did he die?"

"Yep," said King.

Raine's head shot over to him. "You happy about that?"

"Yep, they killed TJ!"

"The drive-by shouldn't have happened."

"Whatever, man. You know how the game goes," said King.

"We don't have to kill each other."

"We don't? It's survival of the fittest for us in the hood. Nobody gives a damn about how we live," said King.

"We don't need other people. We need to care about each other."

"But we don't, and I have a dead father to prove it," King yelled, his chest heaved.

Raine looked away. King was right. No one looked out for him except Mrs. Kathy and King.

"You're right," said Raine.

King relaxed. "I thought you liked Laila."

Raine looked over at King but ignored him.

"Why did you ignore her? She was trying to get your attention in the hallway."

"I'm not worried about that girl," said Raine.

"Whatever. You know you like her."

Raine pulled the door open to the shop and walked over to Dizzy. Dizzy tossed him and King a duffle bag.

"We need to sell all of this. I need y'all on the corner from sunup to sundown," said Dizzy.

"What about school?" asked Raine.

"What about it?" asked Dolla.

Raine turned back at the sound of his voice. Dolla had a way of entering a room without anyone noticing.

"I *said* what about school?" Dolla repeated.

"I can't go to school if I have to stand on a corner all day," said Raine.

Dizzy walked over to Raine and snatched him up. "You run your mouth too much. Get the bags and meet me outside."

"No, I'm going to school."

"Let him go to school," said Dolla.

Relieved he didn't have to miss school or push drugs in the neighborhood, Raine started to walk away.

"But take these with you. I expect y'all to sell all of this. I don't care where you do it," said Dolla.

"I'm gonna quit school," said King.

"Na, push your stuff at school with Raine. This may be some untapped business," said Dizzy.

King snatched the bag and pushed past Raine. Raine thought the crew would end after TJ's death, but The Family moved on. TJ was Dolla's cousin and he hadn't mentioned anything about TJ. Raine realized how replaceable he was to the gang. He didn't want his face on a T-shirt, like TJ, while they continued to do the same thing that caused his death. He had to get out.

∞

Raine walked past another teacher and felt like she could tell he was up to no good. He was trying to make it through the day without anyone finding out he had drugs. He didn't plan on making Dolla or Dizzy a penny. He clenched the strap of his book sack and rushed to first period. He relaxed at the sight of the door. He stared at the floor to avoid Laila's eyes.

"Hi," said Laila. She stopped writing and

watched him until he took a seat.

Raine put his head down on the desk and closed his eyes. He felt a light tap on his shoulder. He glared at her but softened his face when he saw her pout.

"I don't feel like talking," said Raine. He had been ignoring her since she dissed him.

"Ok." She stared at him for a while. "Are you still my friend?"

Raine shrugged.

"Do you wanna come over after school?" asked Laila.

"I don't know."

"Please."

"Alright."

The rest of the class started filing in. Raine almost fainted when he saw King sell weed to another student right in front of the teacher's desk; everyone saw.

"Anybody else wanna cop?" asked King.

"Are you stupid?"

King walked past his desk. "What? We have to sell it. You messed up our chances of being corner boys."

Raine narrowed his eyes at King. They had to sell drugs at school, but King was being reckless. He was already scared, and King wasn't helping. Laila glanced back at him, causing him to look away. Raine heard King make another sell in the back of the classroom. He closed his eyes and pulled out his sketchbook; flipping to a blank page, he drew King in his true form.

∞

Raine slapped his sketchbook on the table and took a seat at one of the computers. His mother was still gone which made him wonder why she was a drug addict. He typed in his grandmother's name, Raeann Landry, to see if anything would show up.

A headline read: Beloved Teacher Gunned Down in Chicago's Westside

He read the article and couldn't believe it. His grandmother was a schoolteacher in Chicago. She was originally from New Orleans but moved to Chicago to teach at one of the toughest schools. The article praised her for being a local hero to kids. The article even mentioned that she was survived by an eight-year-old daughter, Latisha Raeann Landry, and a husband, William Landry.

That explained why his mother was always quizzing him about random stuff. He used to believe that his mother knew everything. Raine searched William Landry. Maybe his grandfather was still alive somewhere.

"This is exactly why we have to sell this stuff at school. You'd rather be in the library like a lame instead of pushing this stuff like me," said King.

Raine ignored him and continued to search for his grandfather. King grabbed the sketchbook off the table, knowing that was the best way to get his attention.

"You have five seconds to put my stuff down."

King smirked and flipped to the last page. He

looked up at Raine. "Is this me? You drew me as a clown? Does it look like I juggle? Do I look stupid to you?"

Raine stood and walked over to King. King's hair was frizzy and some of his braids were coming undone. He always had a fresh set of braids to match his new clothes. Now, his shirt and pants were wrinkled. Raine wondered what was going on with him. Wondering if King looked this rough this morning and how did he miss it.

Raine snatched his sketchbook. "Why are your clothes wrinkled?"

King punched him and grabbed him in a headlock. Raine tossed him off and onto the computers. He punched King in the mouth, drawing blood.

"What's going on in here?" asked the librarian.

King wiped his mouth. "You're gonna need me again. You know you always need a handout."

Raine sighed. He logged off the computer after coming up empty on his grandfather's whereabouts.

∞

Raine apologized to Mrs. Kathy. She gave him a canvas and paint then told him to put his struggles on the canvas. He let Laila convince him to catch her bus and get off at her house. She talked his ear off about any and everything. Raine didn't mind, he liked looking at her while she talked.

She entangled their arms. "What are you gonna paint?"

Raine's body tightened until he looked down at his uniform, it was as clean as hers. "I don't know yet."

He looked across the street and saw a kid learning how to ride a bike. He almost tripped when he saw Jackson was running next to the boy. The boy fell and whined. Jackson scooped him into his arms and hugged him. He carried the boy in one arm and pulled the bike along with the other. Raine's face contorted. *How could he torture me, but be loving and gentle with the boy?*

"I'm sorry your mama is a crackhead."

Raine stopped watching Jackson and pulled his head back. "Huh?"

Laila quickly covered her mouth with her hands. "Sorry."

"I never had anyone apologize to me for my mama."

"I'm sorry I said that."

"It's cool."

Laila opened the front door and threw her jacket down. "Grandma! I'm home."

"What did I tell you about all that hollering in…Hi, Raine," sang Millie.

"Don't switch up now. Show Raine how mean you are to me," said Laila.

Millie laughed. "Gone girl."

She pulled Raine in for a hug. "How you doin', baby?"

The rhythm in her voice settled his thoughts. *Was my Grandma like her?*

"Good."

She took the dish towel off her shoulder. "That's nice to hear. Well, go on and I'll call y'all for dinner."

When Raine walked into Laila's room. She was already on the bed lying on her stomach. She had kicked off her shoes and put the TV on.

Raine removed his supplies from his book sack and prepared his canvas.

"Is it okay if I paint in here?"

"Yeah. I can get a sheet or something to put down."

Raine pulled a drip cloth from his book sack. "Got it covered."

"I swear you keep your book sack full of stuff. Like the Barney bag."

"Barney? You don't know nothing about Barney."

Laila laughed. "I used to have that show on DVD."

"That purple thing was the first thing I learned to draw," said Raine. "That's my dog."

"You mean dinosaur." Laila fell back laughing at her own joke.

"You need help."

He pulled a large paint brush from his book sack and knocked a few bags of drugs out. He picked them up and stuffed them into his book sack. He looked over at Laila and followed her attention to the bag.

She moved from the bed. "So, the rumors are true?"

Raine fumbled with the paint. "What rumors?"

She walked over and sat next to him. "That you are a part of a gang. The Family."

Raine kept quiet.

She exhaled. "I can't picture you being that dumb, but you are."

"I'm not dumb."

"Whatever." She moved to her desk and slammed her notebook on top. She had her back facing him as she mumbled insults.

"You're dumb for wearing that stupid chain," Raine mumbled.

He didn't owe her an explanation. Especially since she was still wearing that chain. Raine decided to ignore her. After sketching, he started painting. He needed water for his brush but refused to asked Laila. He wiped his hand on the cloth and stood to leave the room.

"You're leaving?" she asked.

Raine went to the kitchen. Millie was humming as she stirred a pot; gumbo filled the air.

"Ma'am?"

Millie turned and smiled at the sound of his voice. Raine hadn't noticed her gold teeth until then. "What's wrong, baby?"

"May I have some water for my paint brush."

"Yes, you may and maybe you can teach that child some manners."

Raine smiled.

After getting the water, he returned to the room. He almost knocked Laila over when he pushed the door open. She did a little skip after being caught.

He looked at her and then the door. "Nosey

self."

"I was…"

"Being nosey!" Raine sat on the floor. He painted the last part and dropped his brush. Laila walked over to get a look at his painting. Raine moved it away from her view.

"Really? I can't see?"

"Nope."

She frowned. "Why not?"

Raine twisted his hair. He wasn't sure how she would react to the picture. "It's personal."

"Ok." She pretended to walk away but jumped under his arm and looked at the picture.

Raine moved the picture away after she stared at it and didn't say a word. He laid it on the floor and started packing his supplies.

"Are you leaving?" she asked.

"Yeah."

"Why?"

"It's getting late."

"It's only four o'clock."

Laila kneeled on the floor next to the painting, but she still hadn't said a word about the picture. Raine had painted a picture of her with a gold chain around her neck that read "Raine" in bold letters. He pulled his book sack on his back and turned to Laila. She had moved to the bed and was staring down at her hands.

"Do whatever you want with the picture. Matter of fact…" He snatched it off the ground and threw it in her trashcan by the door. The canvas was hanging halfway out the little trash can. For good measure, he also threw his gold chain in the trash.

∞

Raine came home to an empty house after leaving Laila's. He pulled five hundred dollars from his book sack and waited for Latisha to return. He planned to go pay the bills and drag her along, high or not. He waited on the porch for her until dark then decided to go look for her.

His first stop was a crack house a few blocks away. He stepped on glass vials as he walked up the steps. He was about to push the door open, but someone pulled it opened. A guy flew out and landed next to his feet.

"Try to steal from me?"

A man appeared from the house with a dingy T-shirt on. His eyes were wide and dashed back and forth. He wiped his nose and punched the guy on the ground. Raine eased by them and made his way into the dark house, tall flames from lighters lit the rooms.

He walked past addicts getting high, sleeping on the floor and some were rocking back and forth. A hand plopped on his shoulder making him jump. He quickly shook the hand off and turned around.

"What you doin' in here, boy? You know your mama wouldn't want you in here," said Dennis.

"I'm looking for her. She didn't come home last night."

Dennis clapped his hands together. "Try the house over on Baltimore Street."

"Thanks," Raine rushed out the house and

fanned his nose. The smell from the house had him nauseated. He dry-heaved until he was a few houses down. Baltimore Street was further away but he knew the route like the back of his hand. He had been searching crack houses for his mother since he was eight years old.

The house on Baltimore Street was empty except for a few guys drinking on the porch.

"She ain't here."

"You know where she is?" asked Raine.

The man shook his head. "You have ten dollars?"

Raine sighed but reached into his pocket and handed him twenty. Each time he came to this house the guy always pointed him in the right direction. Raine trekked down the steps and headed for the bus stop. The other houses were on the other side of the city.

"Ay Dreadhead! Try the ninth."

Raine nodded and continued to the bus stop. After paying his fare, he sat at the back of the bus and pulled out his sketchbook. He tapped the pen on his book.

"I told you that was him."

Raine looked up and sunk into his seat. Lewis and his friend were headed to his seat.

Lewis slapped his notebook onto the floor. "What's up now?"

Raine picked his book off the floor and turned his attention to the window.

"Scary," said Lewis' friend.

Lewis tugged on Raine's shirt. "You clean up

nice."

Raine slapped his hand away. "Don't touch me."

Lewis elbowed his friend. "He took a shower and now he doesn't want anyone to touch him. You're still dirty."

"What's going on back there?" asked the bus driver.

Raine walked past them.

"I have two dollars. Do you think your mama can work with that?" asked Lewis.

Raine threw his sketchbook down and rushed Lewis. He was getting the best of him until his friend jumped in. He threw Raine to the floor and they started kicking and punching him until the bus driver threatened to call the police.

The driver pulled the bus over and helped Raine off the floor. "Are you okay, son?"

Raine stumbled to his feet and wiped blood from his face.

"You might need stitches. Let me call the ambulance. Sit down."

Raine pushed him away. "I'm good. Where are we?"

"A few blocks from Ninth Ward."

"Thanks." Raine stumbled down the aisle removing his shirt to wipe the blood.

"Is this yours?" The driver held up his sketchbook.

"No, throw it away." Raine walked off the bus and headed for the house.

The empty beer bottles and glass vials led the way, like the yellow brick road. Instead of searching for a wizard, he searched for his drug addicted mother. The city had condemned the house. The windows and front door were boarded up and the wood was stamped with "No trespassing" signs. A feen slid the wood to the side and entered the house.

Raine wiped blood from his head and headed up the porch. He lifted the board and was about to enter until he heard someone yelling his name.

"What are you doing down here?" Dizzy exited a car wearing all black.

"Looking for my mama."

Dizzy grabbed his shirt. "Your mama? You need to be looking for a hospital. What happened to you?"

"I got jumped."

"By who?" asked Dizzy.

"Don't worry about it. I'll deal with them."

Dizzy stared at him for a second then glanced at the house. "Come on."

"I'm good. I don't need you coming with me. I don't need your help!"

Dizzy jumped at Raine, causing him to raise his fists.

"What's up? I'm not scared of you," yelled Raine. He quickly wiped a tear away.

Dizzy ran his hand down his face. He pulled up his sagging pants then let them fall back to the original position. He walked up the porch and turned back to Raine. "You going to cry all night or come look for her?"

Raine stomped up the porch and ducked under

the wood.

"Y'all stank!" yelled Dizzy.

"Yo mama," one of the addicts yelled.

Dizzy spun around and asked them to repeat it. He threatened to beat them up but couldn't figure out who said it because it was dark.

"I can't see," said Raine.

Dizzy turned on the light from his phone and lit the way.

"Why didn't you respond to the text I sent?" asked Dizzy. "I have to teach you work ethic too?"

"My phone is dead and dealing drugs isn't real work." Raine thought Dizzy was crazy. He thought rules from a legal job applied to dealing drugs.

"Like it or not it's a job and you need to respond to all board meeting texts," said Dizzy.

"Board meeting? Are you crazy?" asked Raine.

"Why didn't you charge your phone?"

Raine ignored him and checked inside a room. He closed the door back when he didn't see his mother. Dizzy slapped him in the back of his head.

Raine rubbed his head. "I don't have any power at home and forgot to charge it at school. If you hit me again, I'll kill you."

"Whatever. This is the last room," said Dizzy.

Raine released a deep breath before opening the door. Dizzy shined the light around the room.

"She isn't here," said Raine.

They walked back onto the porch and Raine stared off into the distance.

"You wanna look some other place?" asked Dizzy.

Raine shook his head. "I checked every house she goes to."

"Hop in and I'll drop you off at home."

"I'm good."

"I wasn't asking." Dizzy walked over to his car and got in.

Raine followed and hopped in on the passenger side.

"How's the work moving at the high school?"

"I haven't sold anything," said Raine.

"Why not? King said he made $2,000 already."

"I don't know, man. I don't even know how to sell the stuff."

"Simple, put the word out that you have some product."

"Ok."

"So, you still got all of it?" asked Dizzy.

Raine snatched his book sack off the floor and opened it. "I have every bag. I don't go anywhere without my book sack. I sleep with it under my head. You don't need to worry about my crackhead mama stealing your stuff!"

"You better calm down. Emotional," said Dizzy.

Raine stared out the window and recognized the area. It was where he painted the wall and got in the newspaper and the place where they did the drive-by.

"Stop." Raine hopped out the car and ran to the wall. The wall was decorated with bullet holes. Mrs. Kathy was trying to do something that brought pride to the neighborhood and the drive-by re-enforced the stereotype of black people in the city.

And he was part of the problem. Raine backed away from the wall and got back in the car.

"Are you crazy? This is enemy territory."

"They're not my enemy," said Raine.

"You painted that, huh?"

"Yeah."

Dizzy shrugged. "You can always paint another."

"I'm done with painting," said Raine.

Dizzy turned the music up and they rode in silence to Raine's house.

"Thanks."

Dizzy didn't offer a response. He simply drove off. Raine dreaded going into the pitch-black house. There was an eerie silence when his mom wasn't home.

CHAPTER 10

Raine waited for his mother all night and was disappointed when he woke to find her still gone. She had never stayed away for more than one day. Today was day four. Raine planned to search for her after school.

Mrs. Kathy had assigned them the task of painting a portrait of a person that inspired them.

"Why haven't you started?" asked Laila. She surprised Raine when she walked into the class with his chain on. Everyone asked if they were dating and she told them *yes*.

Raine couldn't believe someone so beautiful liked him enough to look past his dirty clothing and unkempt hair.

"I'm done with art."

"Done?" Laila asked.

"Raine?"

Raine turned to Mrs. Kathy and saw her standing at the door with two policemen. She looked just as scared as he felt.

"Pack your things. We need you to come with

174

us."

Raine scanned the room for an escape. The windows were across the room and the police were blocking the other exit.

"Let's go, now."

Raine slowly stood. He saw Laila slide his book sack under her legs.

"Give me my book sack."

He didn't need her taking the rap for him. He got himself into this and didn't want her involved. Laila handed her book sack to him. Raine was about to get the right bag but the policeman yelled for him to exit.

Mrs. Kathy followed them into the hallway. "What is this about?"

"We had a surprise shake down and our dogs found drugs in Mr. Landry's locker along with a few thousand dollars."

Raine stopped. "I never use my locker. I haven't used it since the first day of school. Those drugs aren't mine."

The officer pushed him in the back. "Keep walking."

"Wait a minute! What's going to happen to him? He's one of my brightest students," said Mrs. Kathy.

"He'll be brought down for questioning. He's charged with possession of illegal substance on school property with intent to sell. I'll be honest with you, the amount of drugs we found can land him five years in juvie."

Mrs. Kathy stopped walking and grabbed her

chest. Raine followed the cops with his head hung low. He knew the drugs and money weren't his. The drugs he was given were still in his book sack and that was in the classroom. Raine wanted to plead his case. He wanted to tell the officers that they had made a mistake. He wanted to remove the disappointment from Mrs. Kathy's face. Raine opened his mouth but closed it. They wouldn't believe him anyway.

In the back of the police car, he leaned his head on the bar window and watched the city fade. *Maybe my path was preplanned.* He had a drug addicted mom, an absent father, he was poor, he was physically abused and neglected. He felt dumb for even fighting to exist.

∞

The policeman handed Raine a cold drink. "Are you sure there's no one you can call?"

Raine's body was shivering in the ice-cold holding room. He had three unopened cans of cold drink in front of him and a honey bun. Raine had refused all their food and drinks since walking into the room three hours ago.

"Positive."

"Then it's juvie for you until someone can come sign for you to be released to them." He walked out the room and the lock clicked once it closed.

Raine was tired of the sound and the coldness. He wanted to go home, even if it was to lie on a hard floor with scurrying rats. He thought about calling Mrs. Kathy but didn't know her number. She would have come to the station if she was worried. He knew his mother hadn't returned home and he had no way of reaching her.

"Raine, let's go."

Raine followed the officer. He uncuffed him and brought him to a window to get his book sack; well Laila's book sack.

The officer motioned. "You can sign right here. The office will call with more information."

Dizzy pushed past Raine and signed the paper. The officer went around the counter to make a copy for Dizzy.

Dizzy looked around then whispered, "Boy, stop looking at me all stupid."

He knew Dizzy was underage. He wondered how he got the police to release him. Raine turned his attention to the ground. They walked through the hall and Raine heard a familiar voice.

"He's the one that got my child involved in this drug stuff. You should be charging him for all this mess. King didn't get into none of this until he started hanging with Raine."

"Ma'am, calm down."

Raine walked into the room. "I got him in this? He's the cause of all of this. You begged me to help him!"

Dizzy pulled Raine from the room as he tried to get over to King's mother.

When they finally got outside, Raine let out a scream filled with agony and pain. He sat down on the steps and dropped his head in his hands.

Dizzy gave him a minute then tugged on his shirt. "Get up, man."

"Leave me alone."

Dizzy snatched him up and dragged him to his car.

"Why would you leave that in your locker?" Dizzy asked once they were inside the car.

"I didn't. I still have my packs in my book sack."

Dizzy reached down and opened the book sack. "Empty."

Raine sighed. "This isn't my book sack. My girlfriend switched it when the cops came."

"Girlfriend? Where does she stay?"

"Why?"

"Look, right now isn't the time to be questioning me. Dolla wants you and King..."

Raine opened the door and ran out the car. He ducked down an alley and raced away from Dizzy. He ran faster when he heard Dizzy yelling his name. He stopped to catch his breath. He was about to walk across the street but ducked back into the alley. Dizzy slowly drove down the street. As soon as he was farther down the street, Raine dashed across and into another alley.

He walked up to Laila's house and headed to her window. He knocked lightly. The light flicked on and Laila slowly walked to the window.

"It's Raine."

She opened it and let him slide in.

"I need my book sack."

Laila went into her closet and grabbed his book sack. She handed him the bag and jumped into his arms.

"Are you okay? Why are you so sweaty? I thought they were gonna send you to jail."

"I'm good. I'll see you tomorrow." He turned to leave back out the window.

"Promise?"

"Yes. Lock the window back."

When he reached his block, Dizzy was parked out front his house. Raine crept through the backyard and eased through his window.

He sat under the broken window and listened to the wind whistle through. The moon and stars lit the room enough for him to see the puddle of tears on the floor. One of Latisha's hugs wouldn't make his problems go away, but it always made him feel better. He drew his knees up, wrapped his arms around his legs and continued to cry.

∞

Raine was still sitting in the same spot. The sun was shining bright and his room was getting hotter. He hadn't retrieved his bucket to bathe and still had on his school clothing from yesterday. He heard the bus pass earlier and he didn't feel any need to be on the bus. He wanted to stay inside and sleep all day.

He heard pounding on the door. He wiped sweat from his forehead and groaned. Raine knew whoever was knocking was only bringing more trouble. Nothing good ever came through his front door.

He decided to ignore the knocking. He heard the knob click and the door open. Raine held his breath as footsteps got closer. He heard his mother's door open and was happy she was finally home. He was surprised when Jackson burst through the door. Raine tried to get up but Jackson knocked him back down.

"Where's Latisha? I need my money!"

Jackson stood over him with red eyes. Beads of sweat formed on his forehead.

Raine tried to stand again but Jackson shoved him down. "I don't know where she is."

Jackson paced around the room. When he turned his back Raine grabbed his book sack and ran to the door.

"Get back here!"

Raine grabbed the knob but was pulled back by Jackson. Jackson tossed him across the room. His book sack landed on side of him. Raine crawled toward the bag and tried to grab the straps. Jackson walked over and pushed him away. He unzipped the bag and Raine watched his eyes buck.

"I'll just take this."

"No! Those drugs belong to Dolla."

"Tell your crackhead mama I'm looking for her. We were supposed to get high together and she disappeared on me."

Raine punched the floor, deciding to get the bag back from Jackson. He jumped off the floor and ran out the door to find him. He ran next to Jackson and grabbed a hold of the bag. Jackson tried to push him off but Raine only tightened his grip. Jackson choked him and continued to pull the bag away. Raine felt himself fading and his grip loosened. Jackson's face danced from side to side as he dipped in and out of consciousness.

"What are you doing to that boy?" Raine heard as he blacked out.

Raine jumped and looked around. He sat up and dusted off his pants.

"You okay?"

Raine looked over at Dennis. "Yeah."

Raine rubbed his neck. He glanced around and realized he was now on the porch. He stumbled down the steps. "I need to get my book sack back. Did you see where Jackson went?"

Dennis tossed him the book sack. "He took off when I walked up."

Raine unzipped the book sack and made sure the drugs were there. He relaxed when he found everything. He noticed a set of keys and a small bag filled with white powder.

"Did you put these keys in here?"

"Naw, must be for Jackson."

"Thanks, man," said Raine.

Dennis clapped his hands. "Did you find Latisha?"

"No, not yet."

"Keep looking. You got twenty dollars for some liquor?"

Raine reached in his book sack and pulled out

forty dollars.

Dennis snatched the money. "Jackson just mad that Latisha copped and didn't share with him. She left him standing in an alley. Watch yourself, boy. Latisha will turn up."

Raine nodded but his faith in his mother was fading with each day she didn't return.

∞

Raine had stayed in the house for the past three days but needed food. He walked into Mr. Johnson's store and headed down the aisle. Like always, the items he needed were huddled together on the third row.

"You look mighty sad for someone with real money this time," said Mr. Johnson.

Raine counted off five hundred dollars. "Does this cover everything I stole?"

"Where did you get that?"

"Does it cover my debt?" Raine slammed his hand on the counter.

"You don't have a debt here. My wife sits your stuff out for you every month."

"What?"

"Wherever you got this money…take it back," yelled Mr. Johnson. He yanked off his apron and left Raine at the register holding the bills.

After all that time, Raine thought he was tricking Mr. Johnson and stealing the food. It all made sense now. He walked out the store and someone pushed him in the back.

"Snitch," the boy said. Raine kept walking but

glanced back and saw him on the phone. He turned the corner and ran all the way home.

When he got home, he locked the door and checked the windows. Raine knew Dizzy had to be the one that put the word out about him being a snitch. After putting his food up, he sat on the floor to eat. He decided to wait until dark to go out and look for his mother.

Raine fell asleep and was awaken by the window in his bedroom rattling. He grabbed his book sack and stuck his head out into the hallway. He could see someone trying to force the front door open. The window rattled a little more with each kick on the front door. The crack finally gave way and the window shattered as a few people from The Family ran in through the front door. Raine locked his door and jumped out the window. He ran to the backyard but slid down when he saw two more boys waiting by the back door.

"He's back here," one yelled.

Raine took off through his neighbor's yard and hopped her fence. He could hear them closing in on him. Every time he tried to stop to rest, he would hear them. He saw a house perfect for hiding under. He removed the covering and slid under. His book sack got caught on a nail. He quickly removed it and pulled it free. He grabbed the covering and replaced it over the empty spot. He tried his best to slow his breathing as he watched them walk past him. He could see their shoes only. His heart pounded in his chest. Raine was sure they would hear it beating and find him.

"Let's check the back street."

Raine relaxed and looked around. Under the house was hot, dark, and full of dirt. He had The Family after him because Dizzy believed he snitched. He couldn't go back home because Dizzy gave up his address. He was dirty, hungry, and scared.

Raine stayed hidden under the house until dark. He listened as the family in the house got ready for dinner. He remembered when his mother used to cook every night and tuck him in after. He used a stick to draw in the dirt. He imagined what the family looked like as they ate.

Raine decided he couldn't hide forever. He headed for the levee to clear his mind. When he crossed the street, a car stopped right in front of him. The sound of the brakes squeaking caused him to freeze in place.

"You better not run!"

Raine took off down the street and away from Dizzy. He glanced back and saw that Dizzy had parked his car and was out chasing him. Raine ducked between a few cars then dashed down an alley. He made sure to zig zag through the backyards. He squeezed between two houses and waited.

Dizzy yelled his name. "Raine, I swear when I catch up with you, I'm gonna slap them dreads right out your head. I know you hear me!"

Raine waited a few minutes before heading out. He realized he wasn't far from Laila's house. He decided to head there.

Raine lightly tapped on Laila's window. She opened it and he slid inside.

She tried to hug him, but he pushed her away.

She frowned. "What?"

"I'm dirty and sweaty. I haven't bathed all day."

Laila pushed his arms down and hugged him tight. "I don't care."

Raine had his hands down to his side. He closed his eyes then slowly wrapped his arms around her. He sniffed and wiped tears away.

"Are you okay?" Laila asked.

Raine shook his head. Laila kissed his lips.

"I pictured you kissing me on the levee or something." He looked down at his clothes, "Not like this."

Laila led him to her bed. "You want me to wake my grandma? She always fixes my problems or helps me figure out how to fix them."

"No. I'm good. Can I stay here tonight?"

Laila glanced away.

"It's cool if you say no," said Raine.

"You can stay. Just give me a second."

Laila left the room and was gone for a while. Raine was getting nervous and was about to leave. He had the window up with one leg out when she returned.

"Where are you going?" she whispered, then locked the door.

"I was leaving. What took you so long? You didn't tell your grandma, did you?"

"No. I fixed you a sandwich and got some of my brother's clothes from his room."

Raine scoffed down his sandwich as Laila watched him. "What?"

"What kind of trouble are you in?" she asked.

"The Family thinks I snitched when I was at the station."

"Did you?"

"No! I didn't say a word. All I told them was the truth. The drugs and money weren't mine."

Laila nodded. "I believe you."

Raine exhaled. "I think my mama is in trouble. She's been gone for too long. She never goes more than two days without coming back."

Laila gasped. "Maybe you should check the hospital or go to the police."

Raine cut his eyes at her. "The police will only ask questions I don't have the answer to."

"What about the hospital?"

"Maybe," he said.

"I can go with you to check your house for her tomorrow. Maybe she came back."

"I can't go home. The Family sent people there earlier."

"To your house? How do they know where you live?"

"Dizzy; he dropped me off once."

She frowned. "Dizzy?"

"Yeah. You know him?"

"Dizzy is friends with my brother. Are you sure you don't want my grandma's help? My brother and Dizzy hang together. Although my brother says he's not part of The Family, I know he is because he brought me there one morning before school."

"The first time I saw you," said Raine.

"You were there?"

"Yeah, I let King talk me into going to the shop. What's your brother's name?"

"Dorian Junior."

"I never heard of him," said Raine.

"The shower's right there. I can wake my grandma for you or call my brother."

"No, I don't want y'all involved."

After he showered, Raine laid on the floor beside Laila's bed. Laila continued to try and convince him to let her Grandma help, but he refused.

∞

The sun shined through the window waking him up. He sat up and noticed Laila's bed was empty. He smiled when he saw the picture he painted of her hanging above her bed. He noticed her door was open. He walked over to the door and heard Laila whispering.

"He needs help, Grandma. The Family has been chasing after him all day. He thinks his mama's hurt. He can't go home because they know where he lives."

"That poor child," said Millie. "You should've told me sooner. Where is he?"

"Asleep in my room."

Raine's heart sunk. He told Laila that he didn't want her grandma involved. He didn't want the gang coming after them. Her brother was probably low level and didn't have any influence over the gang. Especially, with a name like Dorian.

Raine grabbed his things and hurried through the window, ripping the shirt in the process. He slipped and fell into a muddy puddle. Raine stayed down for a minute contemplating if he wanted to keep running around. He jumped to his feet when he heard Laila's voice.

Raine ran until he saw a restaurant. He dashed into the bathroom and locked the door. He went into a stall and slid down the wall. He kicked his book sack away. The book sack was filled with problems. He pulled it back and opened it, grabbing the baggie of powder Jackson left behind.

He wondered what was in the stuff to make his mother forget to love and care for him. Would the drugs make him forget his problems?

He opened the bag and held it up to his face. He remembered the words his mother wrote in his sketchbook. She told him to fight when life knocked him down. He had fought his whole life and was tired. Each time he was knocked down or picked on, he fought. He fought to merely survive. He was tired of stealing food and water. He was tired of fighting off rats at night. Tired of his mother selling his things. Tired of her being high for days and not checking on him. He fought to dream. He fought to convince himself that his artwork would provide a better life. He fought for

Laila and he fought for King. He fought for his mother time after time. Latisha had given up the fight long ago and now he was doing the same.

He closed his eyes and looked up to the ceiling. "I'm done fighting." He spread the powder onto his finger.

"Why is the door locked." Someone knocked on the door. "Is anyone in there?"

Raine dropped the bag and powder danced to the floor. He heard the person tell the cashier that the door was locked. He flushed the bag down the toilet. He dusted off his pants and eased out the restaurant. He didn't know where to go, so he started towards his house.

Raine knew heading for his house was a bad idea but maybe his mother returned. Besides, he didn't have anywhere else to go. When he got on the street, he locked eyes with King. Instead of walking over to him, King looked away and walked into his house. Raine went into his house and checked his mother's room. Her room was empty. He moved the broken door aside and walked out onto the porch. Someone punched him in the face, causing him to fall to the ground.

"That's for having me chase you around this city." Dizzy snatched him off the ground and dragged him to the car. Raine was kicking and trying to get away.

"Keep still, stupid," said Dizzy.

"Let me go!"

Dizzy threw him inside and put the child lock on the door. Raine elbowed the door while Dizzy rounded the car. He tried to jump into the backseat before Dizzy could open the door. Dizzy hopped in and grabbed his shirt, pulling him back into the front seat.

Dizzy opened the glove compartment and pulled a gun from it. "Shut up and stop jumping around. You're getting mud all over my seats."

Raine was prepared to go to the shop and let The Family do whatever they wanted to him. He was done fighting. He stopped moving and sat still.

Dizzy drove for a few minutes and pulled into a suburb. He drove down a gravel road and killed the engine.

Dizzy held the passenger door open. "Get out my whip."

Raine remained seated, causing Dizzy to yank him out. He pulled Raine out the car and dragged him to the door. He unlocked the door and pushed him in.

"I'm tired of you pushing me around!" Raine shrugged him off.

"I'm tired of you pushing me around," Dizzy mocked, then laughed.

He walked into the kitchen leaving Raine in the living room. Raine heard the microwave go off. He barged into the kitchen and saw Dizzy sitting down to eat. He mugged Dizzy, wondering how he could eat at a time like this.

"Why am I here? Aren't you gonna bring me to The Family?"

"Should I?"

"You tell me. You're the one that told everyone

that I snitched and where I lived!"

"You better calm down. I didn't tell them anything. I've been looking for you since your stupid self jumped out my car."

"If you didn't tell them I snitched and where I live then who did?"

Dizzy shrugged. "I don't know."

"Did you bring me out here to kill me?"

"Why would I kill you in my house. I'm not messing up my carpet. You want some noodles?"

"Man, I can't eat right now," said Raine. He opened his bag and looked at the drugs. Every bag was there. He refused to sell it at school, and he was happy he hadn't made Dolla any money like King did. *King*.

Raine jumped up from the table, scaring Dizzy.

"Boy!" Dizzy pulled his hand back, ready to slap him on the head.

"Wait!" Raine ducked and covered his head. "King. It was King. He was at the station when we left, remember?"

Dizzy sat down. "Yeah."

"Look, I didn't wanna sell drugs at school. I didn't wanna sell drugs at all because of my mama. Every bag is here. The police said they got the drugs out my locker, but it wasn't mine because mine was in my book sack. Remember I told you that my girlfriend switched our book sacks before the police pulled me out of class?"

"Your imaginary girlfriend?" Dizzy turned his lip up.

"I'm not making her up. Her name is Laila

Mitchell."

"Laila Mitchell?"

"Yeah," Raine said. "I bet King put the drugs and money in my locker. I bet he told them where I live and that I snitched too."

Raine paced around the table. "Wait, this is your house?"

"Yep."

"Anyway, I need to get to the shop," said Raine. He had to fix every lie King told. Raine didn't think his life could be any worse, but thanks to King he was longing for his previous problems. They were mild compared to his problems now.

"Tomorrow. I'm tired from chasing after your broke brain self." He pushed back from the table "Don't think about running again. Pick a room and go to sleep."

CHAPTER 11

Raine blinked his eyes.

"Rise and shine, sweetie."

"Ma?" asked Raine.

He slowly opened his eyes. Dizzy slapped his face. "I'm up!"

Dizzy laughed. "You and your breath. Go shower; we got things to do."

After showering, Raine realized he didn't have any clothes. He walked into the room and saw clothes already on the bed. He twisted his hair. One minute Dizzy beat him up, then he looked out for him. He was happy that he had someone in his corner. Raine got dressed and headed into the living room.

"Dizzy?"

He heard the horn blow outside. Raine locked the door and got into the car with Dizzy.

"About time. Now tell me you have a plan before we go to see Dolla."

"I do. How do you know Laila?" Raine asked.

"Let's just say I know her brudda. I know you're

not checking me."

"I might be."

Dizzy laughed. "I don't want your lil' girlfriend. Now what's your plan?"

"I'm going to show Dolla that I have all of my bags and that I only have the money I made from the jobs we did. If I'm right about King, he won't be able to show his stash because the police have it."

"Cool. Let's go."

"Stop by my house first."

When they pulled up on his block, there were two police cars in front of his house and a van.

"Why are they here?" asked Raine. "Are they here because of the drug charge?"

"You don't have a drug charge. The police that released you works for Dolla. The charge was dismissed. How do you think I was able to sign you out? I'm only sixteen, stupid."

Raine sighed. "Then why are they here?"

Dizzy leaned forward. "That's a state van. It's C.P."

"What's that?" asked Raine.

"It's Child Protection. Someone must have told them about your mama using drugs. Is she home?"

"No. I haven't found her yet."

"Yet? She's still gone?"

"Yeah."

"You can't go home," said Dizzy. "Let's head to Dolla."

When Dizzy pulled up, a few guys were standing outside.

"What's up, Dizzy? I see you found the rat."

"Yeah, now step aside."

"Mr. Raine, you are a hard person to catch," said Dolla.

"I didn't…"

"Get at him," said Dolla.

A few members punched Raine in the stomach and kicked him when he fell.

"Dizzy, get in," said Dolla.

Dizzy walked over to them and punched one of the boys in the face, knocking him out.

"What are you doing?" asked Dolla.

Dizzy pulled Raine off the floor. "He didn't snitch. Let him explain."

"You're going really hard for him," said Dolla. "You knocked poor Dallas out."

"I am and so did Laila. She held his pack for him when the police pulled him from school."

"Laila? My sister Laila?" Dolla asked. "How do you know my sister?"

Raine frowned. "Leave her out of this."

"They go out," said Dizzy.

Raine shoved him. "Shut up."

"Ay, you know your shirt that Jordan signed for you?" Dizzy asked.

"Yeah, I keep it by my grandma's house. For the last time, you can't buy it. It's priceless," said Dolla.

Raine pulled at Dizzy's arm trying to stop him from talking.

Dizzy shrugged him off and laughed. "He was

wearing it yesterday. It's all muddy, dusty and torn in the back."

"How did you get my shirt!" yelled Dolla. He looked like he wanted to faint.

"I...she..."

"I'm gonna kill Laila," said Dolla. "Then, I'm gonna kill you."

"Dizzy, you're not helping!" yelled Raine.

Dizzy threw his hands up and backed away.

"Start talking, Raine," Dolla said.

Raine showed him the drugs and explained to him that King had set him up.

"King was the one that said you snitched and that your mama had stolen your drugs. Ay, somebody get King here. Now!"

Dolla's little henchmen rushed out the door in search of King. Dolla walked up to Raine. "When there's a problem you come to me. Don't run around like a coward. Come to me like a man and explain your problem. You never let another man feel like they have control over your life. You heard me?"

Raine nodded and took a seat next to Dizzy. He dropped his head in his lap.

"Sit up and look confident," said Dizzy.

Raine wiped his eyes and sat up. He wasn't sure if Dolla believed him or not. He didn't know if he would even make it out of the shop. He just wished that his mother was safe, wherever she was.

An hour later, someone threw King through the door. He looked at Raine with a scowl. Raine was off the sofa and rushing toward him. Before he

Raine

reached him, King pulled a gun stopping him in his tracks.

"Put that gun down," said Dolla.

"No, I'm about to end this snitch," said King.

"He's the snitch or you," said Dolla.

"I told you. Raine was the one that told."

"You can kill him...after you give me the packs," said Dolla.

"I don't have it," said King.

"What happened to it?"

"I sold it," said King.

"Cool, give me the money."

"I don't have it."

"You don't have the drugs or the money?"

Dolla walked over to him and stood right next to King. King's eyes dashed from Dolla to Raine.

"No, you don't have it because the police took your stash. Which means you put your stuff in your friend's locker instead of taking the lick. A lick that would've went away because of my connections. You got caught anyway because the dogs found residue on your clothing. They didn't shake down Raine's class, just the English building. You know how I know this? Because I have connections. You put the word out without my permission that he was a snitch. When in fact, I have a tape of your confession. You and your mother gave them information about me and information about Raine's home life. I let you walk around after you snitched on the strength of Royal, but your nothing like your father."

King put the gun down and backed away. He

shot Raine that familiar look. The one that begged for Raine to bail him out, take on his problems or take the fall. Raine mugged him and shook his head.

"No more. I won't fight for you anymore. I don't owe you a thing. I'm paid in full," said Raine.

"Give me the gun. You know you don't have the heart," said Dolla.

King raised the gun and pulled the trigger. Dolla grabbed King and wrestled the gun from his hands. Raine felt Dizzy pulling him away.

"Put him in the car," yelled Dizzy.

"Y'all keep King here," yelled Dolla, as they carried Raine out to Dizzy's car.

"Hold on, lil' brudda," said Dolla.

Raine grabbed his stomach and felt blood dripping through his fingers. Wet like acrylic paint. He turned his hand over and watched the red blood drip down. He closed his eyes.

"Rainbow, stop putting your hand in the paint, use the paint brush."

His mother walked over and wiped his hands off with a dish rag. As soon as she was finished, he stuck his hand right back in the tub of paint.

She laughed. "Okay. I guess we are finger painting."

The sound of her laugh, her face glowing, and the smell of red beans cooking made him not want to leave. The house was bright, and every spot was decorated with furniture or wall art. He was sitting at his little desk in the kitchen. His mother used it to keep him entertained while she cooked.

"We're celebrating something big, Rainbow. Mommy passed her Praxis test. Now, I can start looking for teaching jobs. Are you happy?"

Raine didn't know what that meant but she was happy and that made him happy. So, he nodded his little head and gave her a kiss on the cheek.

Muffled voices shattered his dream. "Keep your eyes open."

He was trying to breathe, but it felt like an elephant was sitting on him. He tried to tell Dizzy, but the words wouldn't leave his mouth. *Was this how TJ felt?*

"Don't talk. Keep your eyes open," said Dizzy.

Dolla got into the driver's seat and pulled away at full speed. "How's he doing?"

"He's gonna be all right. You hear me, Raine." Dizzy shook him.

Raine wanted to believe him but his eyes felt heavier every second. Finally, he gave in and closed them. Dizzy's voice got lower and eventually faded.

CHAPTER 12

"Today, we are covering the event of a thirteen-year-old local student that was shot two months ago. His artwork on display was provided by his art teacher, a local couple that owns a grocery store, a notepad found by a local bus driver and a few other people he met. We have his art teacher here now," said the reporter.

"Afternoon, I want to invite everyone to come down to Garvey High and have a look at the work of a young prodigy. He had potential that we will never see reached," said Mrs. Kathy.

Dizzy cut the radio off as he pulled up to the school. The parking lot was packed with cars. There were three news vans covering the event. A banner with Raine's picture hung outside the door. It was the same one from the newspaper.

He walked around the room looking at the pieces. They had pulled out all the pages in his sketchbook, enlarged them and posted them up on the wall. One of the pictures was of himself. Raine had drawn a picture of Dizzy posted on his car. Dizzy couldn't believe that he fit so much detail on one page. Raine was talented and he was sorry he hadn't realized it until then. He didn't belong in a gang, he belonged in art school. Dizzy felt his eyes water, so he headed for the door.

"Yo, Dizzy, you headed out?" Dolla asked. He had his arm around Laila as she cried.

"Yeah, man. I just stopped by for a second."

"Laila, let me talk to Dizzy for a second."

Dolla raised his shirt and showed the tattooed picture of his mother and TJ that Raine had drawn. "We all feel this one."

Dizzy nodded. "I'm out."

He arrived at the hospital and went up to the fifth floor. Every other day for the past two months, he walked into the dimly lit room. The only sound was the machine beeping. He placed the sketchbook on his table along with the other stack. Every time he visited, he brought a sketchbook. Today's sketchbook made number twenty.

Dizzy sat next to Raine's bed. He sat in silence as he watched his chest move up and down with the help of a life-support machine.

"I found your mama. She's in a rehab center. You couldn't find her because she got arrested. I used to search crack houses for my mama too. She died from an overdose when I was ten. You need to fight to wake up. They're trying to pull the plug on you. You always been stubborn, but I need you to let that stubbornness go and get up."

Dizzy exhaled. He walked to the door and glanced back at Raine's bed."

CHAPTER 13

Dizzy laid flowers on the grave. He leaned down and kissed the headstone. "I wish things would've turned out different."

This day was always depressing for him. It was the day he lost one of the only people he cared about. Dizzy walked through the grass and to his car. He never stayed in the graveyard for long.

"Get your stupid self off my whip."

Raine exhaled. "Nobody's gonna mess up this ugly car."

Raine hopped into the passenger seat and slammed the door. He smirked when Dizzy frowned.

"Keep on," said Dizzy. "You got everything? I'm not going back home."

"I got everything."

They pulled up to Raine's school after Dizzy visited his mother's grave.

"Thanks," said Raine.

He turned back and leaned into the car. "Can you see why my mama hasn't written me back yet?"

"Yeah, yeah, get out. We might drive out there this weekend."

Raine smiled. "Cool."

He adjusted his clothing and made sure his colostomy bag wasn't sticking out too much. He had been wearing it since leaving the hospital. The doctors told him he would have to wear it for over a year while he healed from the gunshot to his stomach. He had to clean it every day and he hated the smell, but he was happy to be alive.

Dizzy took him to his home after he was released. He took care of him like a big brother. One minute Dizzy would slap him around and then the next he would school him. Raine felt nothing but pride every time Dizzy referred to him as his little *brudda*.

"Raine, did you bring my chemistry book?" asked Laila.

"Here."

She kissed him. "Thanks. I wanna study before the test."

"You're the smartest person I know."

She grabbed his hand. "And you're the most talented person I know. Shouldn't you be headed to the art room."

Mrs. Kathy had asked Raine to present his newest piece to a few art professors.

"Yeah, I'll see you later." He hurried to the room and tried to calm his nerves.

"Nice job, kid."

Raine shook each of their hands, firmly, like Mr. Rod taught him.

"You're perfect for our new program for high school artists. Very well-spoken, well-kept appearance. This kid's clothing has more creases on it than my Armani suit."

Raine smiled. Dizzy ironed his clothing each night and bought him shoes before the old ones were worn.

"Thanks," said Raine. "I can't take all of the credit. Mr. Rod helps me elevate my skills with all of the different tips and techniques he's shown me."

"Yes. Roddy meets with Raine twice a week," said Mrs. Kathy.

Raine chatted with the professors for a while then he headed to first period.

"Hey, Raine," sang Essence.

Raine turned up his lip. Essence went from making fun of him and telling Laila to stay away from him to smiling and flirting with him.

"Tell your little brother to see me when he makes eighteen. I still want my round."

He laughed when Essence rolled her eyes. Lewis was right behind her. He mugged Raine when he passed. Occasionally, Lewis would try one of his old jokes. Raine ignored him and anyone else that made fun of him. Even though he didn't wear dirty clothes or walk around with a jacked-up hairline, kids still found ways to clown him.

Raine rushed out of Dizzy's car and over to their mailbox. He looked through the bills for Latisha's letter. He froze when he spotted a letter from a detention center. The letter was addressed to him from *King Brooks*. He walked over to Dizzy. He pushed the mail in his hand and headed into the house.

"Did she write?" asked Dizzy. He shook his head when Raine ignored him.

After a long shower, Raine walked into his room to find the letter from King sitting on his bed. He groaned, wishing Dizzy had thrown it away.

Dizzy knocked on his door. "I'm headed out for a while. You good?"

"Yeah."

"Cool. You know the rules. It's a school night so don't be up all night on the phone with Laila. I'll call when I'm on my way back."

Raine stared at the carpeted floor. Every time Dizzy went to work with Dolla, Raine's stomach would be in knots. He worried about losing him like TJ.

"Look, how about we go see your mama tomorrow evening instead of waiting until Saturday," said Dizzy.

"For real?" Raine's head shot up.

"Yeah. I'll be back, though," said Dizzy.

Raine placed the letter in his drawer, then followed after Dizzy to lock the door.

"Be safe," said Raine.

"Always, lil' brudda," said Dizzy. "Wait. Don't eat my lasagna."

Raine closed the door and headed for the kitchen. He pushed past all the food and found Dizzy's lasagna tucked in the back. He pulled it out, did a little dance and microwaved it.

I can't wait to see my mama, he thought.

∞

Raine stood at the entrance of the school with Laila.

"What do you wanna do for your birthday?"

Raine shrugged. "Don't matter, as long as you, Dizzy and Miss Millie there."

"You know we will be there. There's Dorian. I'll see you later. Give me kiss."

"Girl, you crazy? You don't see your brother staring at us."

"Dorian isn't worried about us," said Laila. She still had her lips puckered.

"Dorian isn't worried about us but *Dolla* looks like he wants to kill me," said Raine.

Laila pouted.

"Cool, my death is on your hands," said Raine, making Laila giggle.

He leaned in to kiss her and Dolla held the horn down.

"Ay!" Dolla shouted.

"I'll call you." Raine rushed out and dashed to Dizzy's car.

He looked in the side mirror to make sure Dolla wasn't headed his way.

Dizzy laughed. "What's wrong?"

"You know what's wrong. Dolla...I mean

Dorian, can't stand me."

"You did ruin his shirt signed by Michael Jordan."

"Man, y'all need to let that go. Plus, Laila grabbed that shirt."

Dizzy waved him off. "You ready to go see your mama?"

Raine buckled his seatbelt. "Yep."

Dizzy pulled off and headed to Baton Rouge. He slapped at Raine's hands when he tried to change the song.

"Don't touch."

"Why can't I listen to something else?" asked Raine.

"My car, my rules," said Dizzy.

Raine pulled out his sketchbook and worked on a picture for his mother.

Two hours later, they were pulling up to the rehab center. Where Latisha had been for the last 7 months. Raine jumped when Dizzy slapped his face.

"Do you ever wake people up like a normal person?"

Dizzy laughed. "Nope."

Raine waited in the visiting area for his mother. He stood when she walked out.

"Hey, Rainbow."

She had gained her weight back and her hair was down to her shoulder. Her smile caused him to smile.

"Hey, Ma."

They hugged. She held him longer than usual.

When she pulled back, her eyes were teary.

"How are you, Wesley?" she asked.

Raine tried to hold in his laugh, but he ended up laughing loud causing the other visitors to look their way. Dizzy hugged Latisha, then tried to get to Raine, who hid behind her. Raine would never get over Dizzy's real name being Wesley Thurman.

"Ok. I'm gonna have my hands full with you two," said Latisha. "Sit down."

"How's everything?" asked Raine.

"Everything is fine. I'll be glad when I'm out of this place."

Latisha had good days and bad days. She was a little down today, which made Raine sad.

"I wrote you."

Latisha patted his leg. "I know. I sent your letter the other day."

She looked at Dizzy. "Wesley, let me talk to Raine alone."

Latisha stared at Raine for a while. She grabbed his hand. "You still twist your hair when you're uncomfortable."

Raine nodded. "I guess. I worry about you, Ma."

"I know." She dropped her head. "I wanted to tell you about your grandfather. When you asked last month, I wasn't ready to tell you. After my mother died, he wasn't the same. He moved us back to New Orleans and barely left the house. When I was in high school, he died."

"How did he die?"

"Overdose," she replied. "I found him after getting off the bus."

Raine exhaled. "Seems like our family is cursed."

"No. You have all of our strengths. My mama's caring soul, my father's quiet demeanor, my smarts, and your father's fight. You remember that note I wrote in your book?"

Raine wiped his eyes. "You said to fight."

Latisha nodded. "Fight, baby. Are you still fighting?"

Raine shook his head. "No." He hadn't been in a fight since his shooting.

"Didn't you wake up from a coma?"

"Yeah."

"Didn't you get that mentorship?" she asked.

"Yeah."

"Didn't you survive without my help?"

Raine nodded. "I am fighting."

Latisha smiled. "You sure are."

They chatted until visiting hours were over. On the drive back home, Raine and Dizzy cracked jokes on each other. Latisha's recovery was bittersweet for Raine, because when she was better, he would have to leave Dizzy and go back home.

For now, he was focused on fighting like his mother said. He was excited about school and seeing Laila. She always wanted to hear about his mother.

∞

Dizzy had picked Raine up from school and they were pulling into the driveway.

"What are we having for dinner?" asked Raine.

"Don't know."

Dizzy had been quiet with him and didn't laugh at his corny jokes. Raine rushed into the house to prepare for Mr. Rod. He was setting up the easel when Dizzy walked in and sat on his bed.

"Sit down."

"Ok. I'm almost done setting up for Mr. Rod."

"I told Mr. Rod not to come today," said Dizzy.

Raine dropped the easel. "Why?"

"Sit down," said Dizzy.

Raine sat next to him and grabbed the letter Dizzy extended.

Dear Family of Latisha Landry...

Raine stared at the words in disbelief. His body felt weak. He ripped the paper and burst into tears.

"Why did she do that?" he yelled. "We just saw her last week."

Dizzy held his head down. "I don't know."

Raine kicked the easel down. "She told me to fight, but she gave up."

His mother found a way to sneak drugs into the facility and had overdosed. She wasn't found until the next morning.

Raine picked up the easel and slammed it on the floor. He slammed the easel again and again; exhausted, he dropped to the floor. The easel was in pieces. Dizzy wiped his eyes on his shirt, and then got on the floor with him, pulling him into a tight hug. Raine cried until he couldn't produce any more tears. Dizzy scooped him up and placed him in the bed. Raine thought he would leave, but Dizzy sat in the recliner next to his bed and stayed there.

The next morning Raine got ready for school. Dizzy tried to convince him to stay home but he needed to get some art done. Latisha wanted him to fight and that's what he was going to do.

"Can you stop at Mr. Johnson's store?"

"Why?"

"Laila's taking her honors placement test and she's nervous. I want to get her favorite snacks."

"Ok, lover boy," said Dizzy.

"Morning Mrs. Johnson, where's that old grumpy man?"

"Hey, Raine, he's out back throwing away trash."

Raine grabbed Laila's snacks and walked up to the counter.

"Hello, Thunderstorm," said Mr. Johnson.

Raine laughed. "Ok. I'll remember that while I'm drawing your portrait."

Mr. Johnson laughed. "Get on out my store, boy."

Raine walked through the parking lot towards Dizzy's car.

"Where's Latisha? She still owes me money."

Raine looked over at Jackson. He held his nose to keep from vomiting. Jackson was so skinny the bones in his face showed.

"You won't be getting anything from her."

"You wanna bet? Where is she?"

"Dead."

Jackson laughed. "Karma for stealing from me."

Raine ran toward Jackson. He continued past Jackson and over to Dizzy. Dizzy had his gun pointed at Jackson.

"I warned you not to come near him." Dizzy tossed Raine to the side and continued over to Jackson. He placed the gun next to his head.

"You wanna repeat what you just said?" asked Dizzy.

"No, Diz. Don't do it," said Raine. He grabbed Dizzy's arm and tried his best to pull him away. Dizzy wasn't budging.

"You're all I got left," said Raine.

Dizzy slowly lowered his gun. Jackson was standing still with his hands up. Dizzy slammed the gun down on Jackson's head knocking him out. Dizzy walked over to his car leaving Raine staring at Jackson. Raine spun around and followed Dizzy. Mr. Johnson gave Raine a nod and walked back into his store.

∞

Raine decided to have a small ceremony for his mother. He had fought back tears at the funeral but broke down when he got home. He had been on the floor in his bedroom for the last two hours. Dizzy checked on him every few minutes, but he never came in or said a word. Raine heard low voices outside his door. He recognized Laila, Dolla, Dizzy and Miss Millie's voices. Everyone tried to whisper, but miss Millie was loud.

"Somebody better go in there and get him out here. He hasn't eaten a thing," she fussed.

There was a soft knock on the door. Laila walked over and sat on the floor next to him. She sat his food on the dresser and hugged him.

"Do you want to draw something?"

Raine shook his head.

Laila grabbed his sketchbook and pencil. A few minutes later, she tapped his arm and gave him the book.

"You took that long to draw this?" asked Raine.

She punched his arm. "Shut up."

Laila had drawn stick figures of them holding hands with hearts around them. She had two little stick figures next to them.

"When my parents died, Grandma told me that it was only a sad moment in time and that I had my whole life ahead of me, and that I'll see them again. I know it's hard to see past your mama's death right now, but I wanna go to the same college as you and then marry you."

Raine heard a noise coming from the door and knew that Dizzy probably had to hold Dolla back from coming in after hearing Laila's confession.

"Can you eat a little food for me?" she asked.

"Maybe later."

"Ok. I'll check on you later."

Laila walked out and Raine heard mumbling again. Next, Dizzy walked in.

"Just give me a minute, Dizzy."

"No. Miss Millie wants you to eat something, and she isn't letting us leave the door until you do."

Raine reached over and grabbed one grain of rice and ate it. "There."

Dizzy laughed. "Bruh, you are annoying."

Dizzy sat on the bed. "You're never going to stop thinking about her. If you're waiting for that to end, you'll be in this room forever."

"I know."

They both turned around when they heard the door open. Dolla walked in rubbing his stomach. He dropped down in the recliner next to Raine's bed.

"Grandma trippin'. We can't eat until you eat. I'm starving," said Dolla.

Dolla grabbed the plate and pushed it in Raine's hand.

"I'm not hungry," said Raine.

"I am. Now, eat the food so Grandma can give me a plate," said Dolla.

Raine stared down at the plate, eating was the last thing on his mind.

"You haven't eaten anything since yesterday. Look around you. We all lost at least one of our parents. You got all this love surrounding you. Your mama told you to fight, right? Do that. Eat your food," said Dolla.

Raine scooped a spoonful of food into his mouth.

"Grandma, he's eating," yelled Dolla.

"Dorian, I told you and your sister about all that yelling," said Millie. "Come in the kitchen everyone."

When they got in the kitchen, Laila kissed Raine.

"Stop kissing my sister, punk."

Laila sighed. "Grandma."

"Dorian, leave them babies alone," said Millie.

Raine smirked at Dolla. Miss Millie was always quick to get on Dolla for picking at him. Dolla shook his fist at him.

∞

After school, Raine left before Dizzy arrived. He went to his old house and saw King's mother sitting on the porch. She rolled her eyes and went into the house.

Raine knew she blamed him for King, but he didn't care. King wasn't his friend and only gave him food because it made Raine a pawn. Raine hadn't read the letter yet, but he knew eventually he would read it.

He jogged up the steps and into the house. His first stop was his mother's old room, but he didn't walk past the doorway. He walked over to his old bedroom before getting emotional. Sitting under the window, he drew his legs up to his chest and pulled out his recent painting. It was a picture of his mom. He leaned it on the wall and wiped his eyes with his shirt.

Everything would be perfect if his mother was alive. For the first time in his life, he felt protected and even loved, but Latisha left a void that no one could fill.

Raine never allowed himself to sulk for too long, so he pulled himself off the floor and left the house. His mother wanted him to fight and he was still doing that. He walked down the porch and saw Dizzy parked out front. Raine knew he would find him. Dizzy always did.

"What do you want for dinner?" asked Dizzy.

"Don't matter. Long as you don't cook," said Raine, making Dizzy laugh.

Thanks for checking out my story. If you enjoyed my book, please leave a review

To connect with me please visit

Facebook: Author Ty Sam-Davis

Twitter: @TySamDavis1

Made in the USA
Columbia, SC
21 July 2021